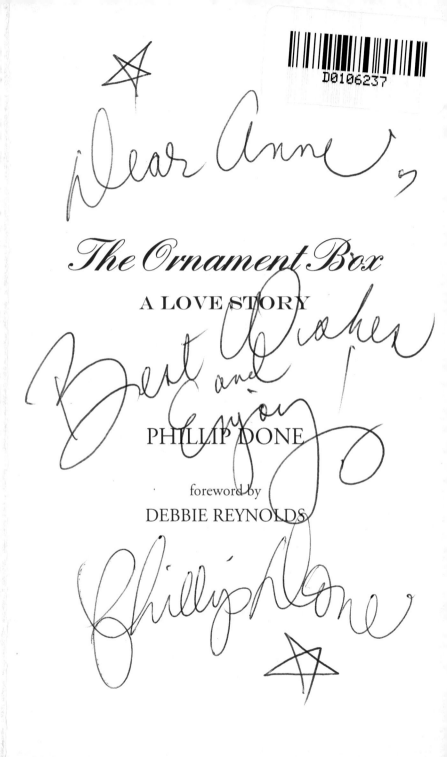

The Ornament Box

A LOVE STORY

PHILLIP DONE

foreword by
DEBBIE REYNOLDS

Dear Anne,

Best Wishes and Enjoy!

Phillip Done

GATEWAY PUBLISHING
Mountain View, CA

Cover Art: Tia Graeff
Cover Design: Brian Halley
Author Photo: Paul Corfield
Interior Design: Polgarus Studio

Manufactured in the United States of America

ISBN-13: 978-1534921627
ISBN-10: 1534921621

This book is lovingly dedicated to the memory of Ann Rutherford.

ALSO BY PHILLIP DONE

32 Third Graders and One Class Bunny:
Life Lessons from Teaching

Close Encounters of the Third-Grade Kind:
Thoughts on Teacherhood

The Charms of Miss O'Hara:
Tales of Gone With the Wind and the Golden Age of
Hollywood from Scarlett's Little Sister

Foreword

When author Phillip Done sent me *The Ornament Box*, I was immediately intrigued. Of all my possessions, one of the most cherished is my box of Christmas ornaments. I imagine most families have one. Big or small, old or new, all year long these boxes sit quietly in attics, basements, or garages. Then one day in December — or sometimes earlier for those like me who are eager to see them — there is the rattle of a stepladder, and the boxes are taken down, carried into warm living rooms, dusted off, and opened up once again on rugs and coffee tables near the Christmas tree.

Lifting the lid off the box is like opening up an old photo album or a well-loved storybook. Every year when I unwrap my ornaments from their tissue paper nests, I can't help but smile. It's like seeing old friends. Each ornament has a history. Each holds a story. My ornament box is not just filled with bulbs and balls and gifts made at school out of empty spools and coffee can lids. It is filled with memories — memories of love and loss, family and faith, home and hope. All ornament boxes are. They are the treasure chests of Christmas.

In this beautiful and moving book, Phillip Done opens his family's ornament box for you. The stories it holds will touch your heart, as they have mine. Come — let's look inside.

Debbie Reynolds

"The violin trembles like a heart betrayed . . ."
— "Evening Harmony," by Charles Beaudelair

Chapter One

I parked the car in front of my parents' place and sat there for a few minutes looking up at the house. It was just past noon on Christmas Eve. I did not want to go inside. Not this Christmas. There were no wreaths on the front door and no lights hanging above the garage. The plastic carolers weren't out on the lawn, and the big wooden Santa that always stood on the roof by the chimney wasn't there either.

Eventually, I got out of the car and walked up the steps. Red and yellow leaves dotted the walkway, and the cement was wet from the morning rain. As I stepped up to the porch, I could hear a hymn playing on the radio. My mother always listened to her gospel station in the afternoon. For a moment, I stared at the plastic white button in the center of the doorbell. I took a deep breath and pressed it. After a few seconds, I knocked on the door. Suddenly, footsteps clicked down the hall, and the lock turned. Mom opened the door with a smile.

"We've received reports from the neighbors that your radio is too loud," I said, grinning.

Mom chuckled and reached out her arms. "Merry Christmas, Michael. I'm so glad you're here." She waved me inside. "Come in. Come in."

I stepped into the house and gave her a bear hug. "Merry Christmas." She smelled like Camay soap. I pulled away and held out a pine wreath with a poofy red bow. "This is for you."

"Oh, it's beautiful."

"Karen made it."

Karen and I had just celebrated our seventh anniversary. We had a five-year-old son named Christopher.

"Be careful where you hang that thing," I warned, smiling. "There's mistletoe in it."

She held the wreath in front of her and thanked me. Then she kissed me on the cheek.

I gave a laugh. "Well, I see the mistletoe's working."

My mom looked like she always did at Christmastime in her red turtleneck, black slacks, and apron with large red and white poinsettias. Her white hair was done up in a French twist fastened with a gold clip. She wore the pearl earrings my dad brought back from Japan when he was in the Navy. Mom was still a beautiful woman. She'd always watched what she ate and walked a lot. When asked her secret, she gave her pat answer: "Lots of fat cells. Better than Botox."

As I took off my coat, I looked into the living room, where a large Douglas fir stood in the center. The tree was bare.

"I thought you weren't getting a tree this year," I said.

"Oh, Mr. Fletcher from church got it for me and brought it over."

"That was nice of him." Then I took in a long breath. "It smells good."

"Thanks for coming early," Mom said.

"No problem."

Mom had called to ask if I would come by before the rest of the family to help with the decorations. Normally, my mother would have had the whole house decked out by then. She always started decorating the day after Thanksgiving. Usually the dishes from Thanksgiving dinner wouldn't even be put away, and Dad would be carrying down the Christmas boxes. But this year, Mom just couldn't get to it.

It seemed odd not to see any decorations anywhere. The fireplace mantel was empty. No candles sat in the windowsill; no carol books rested on the piano. There were no pine branches on the staircase, or red and green Hershey's Kisses in the milk glass candy bowl on the coffee table. Only a basket of Christmas cards sat on the entryway floor. It looked like some hadn't been opened yet.

I put my hand on the banister and looked upstairs. "How is he?" I whispered.

"He's sleeping now."

Back in September, my father began complaining of stomach pain. After Mom nagged him to go see a doctor, he finally went. The doctors ran several tests over the next couple of weeks. It didn't look good, so they took a biopsy. He had stomach cancer. The hospital put him on the surgeon's schedule. The ladies at church put him on the prayer chain.

The news of Dad's cancer shocked us all. Up until then, he had been the healthiest guy I knew. I remember him being sick only once, and even then he wouldn't stay home from work. When my dad was diagnosed, he was playing on three different senior softball teams. He was in better shape than I. He was only sixty-four.

Before the surgery, I hadn't been to my parents' much. My mom often invited me over, but I usually said I was busy with work or writing my dissertation. I taught in the education department at a local college. The truth was — I didn't want to go. My father and

I just weren't that close. When I did stop by, Dad would usually work up in his office while I sat downstairs with Mom, or he'd watch TV in the family room. My father was crazy about sports and sat glued to the set when a game was on. Once in a while, I'd watch a game with him, but I didn't enjoy it. We'd sit in silence, and I'd wonder why I was even there. It was pointless to try and carry on a conversation during a game. When we did speak, it was never for long.

After complaining about it more than once to Karen, she suggested having my parents over for dinner. So we did. But when they arrived, the first thing my father did was turn on the TV. Mom made him turn it off, but by then it was too late. I was angry and hurt. After that, I decided it was easier to just stay away.

Growing up, my dad hadn't been around much either. He worked in finance at a large banking corporation and had his own tax practice on the side, which took up most of his weekends. Because of his work, we rarely went on vacation, and he missed most of my basketball games and band concerts in high school. Over the years, Mom tried to fill in for him. Once, when I was young, she offered to play catch with me, but I declined. When I opened presents from my parents, I knew my dad was seeing them for the first time. On my birthday cards, "Dad" was written in my mother's handwriting. He wasn't a rotten father. Just absent.

There were some good times though. I remember one Saturday morning when I overslept and was late for my paper route. My dad loaded the back of the station wagon with newspapers and drove me all around town. Afterward, he bought me a hot chocolate. Occasionally, he'd bring my sister and me those little snack pack boxes of cereal that you cut open, pour milk into, and eat right out of the box. My mom didn't approve of us eating sugary cereals, but Dad would let us eat the Frosted Flakes and Froot Loops anyway. Once, he took the whole family out to dinner at the A&W, where he ordered the Mama Burger and my mom got the Papa Burger. It made us all laugh. I cherish these memories. Unfortunately, there just weren't enough of them. A son should have more good times with his father than he can count.

The evening Mom called with news of the cancer, I walked into my bathroom, gripped the counter, and started to cry. I turned the faucet on so that Karen and Christopher wouldn't hear me. As the water ran, my chest bounced with tears. Every few seconds, I'd have to inhale sharply, like a drowning man gasping for air. I begged God to heal my father. "Please, God," I cried.

"Dear God, please take the cancer away . . . *please*." I was surprised at my reaction. I didn't expect to respond this way. Leaning over the sink, I realized how much I longed for a relationship with him. And now, I was running out of time.

After wiping my eyes and taking a few more deep breaths, I stood there for a moment staring at my reflection in the mirror. I looked a lot like my dad; I always had. We had the same nose, smile, and eyes. As the tear-stained face looked back at me, it felt like my father had been crying with me.

For weeks, I felt fogged, off balance. One moment I'd be fine, then another I'd find myself fighting back tears. Sometimes, the simplest things would trigger it. One day after the news, I was standing in line at Starbucks when violin music started playing on the speakers. My dad played the violin. I got so emotional that I had to leave the store. Keeping busy helped. I could get through my work all right. It was when I was still that I'd be bombarded by memories of him.

Night was the worst. In bed, I'd lay for hours staring at the ceiling as fractured snapshots flooded my mind — a piggyback ride, his strong hands holding my little ones under the faucet to warm them up after playing in the snow, hearing him run behind me to make sure I didn't fall off my bicycle after the training wheels were removed, seeing him poke his nose into the Thanksgiving turkey after Mom pulled it out of the oven, watching him search for loose change in his pocket to toss into the beat-up case of a street musician. As I lay there in the dark, I'd squeeze my eyes, trying to bring the images into sharper focus. It was as if I were trying to crawl back into them. I missed him already.

After learning of the cancer, I wanted to spend as much time with my dad as I could; I just wanted to be near him. I bought him a La-Z-Boy recliner and set up a hospital bed in his office. A couple of times I drove him to his doctor's appointments to give my mom a break. I was shocked the first time he took off his shirt. His once muscled chest was gone now, and he had trouble raising the arms that used to throw me across the pool. It was difficult seeing him that way.

When my father was recuperating from surgery, I stopped by the hospital every day. (After the doctors opened his stomach to remove the cancer, they just sewed him back up; there was too much of it.) Once in a while, I'd read him the sports page. Occasionally, I would just sit with him while he slept, watching the rise and fall of his chest. Sometimes, I'd find myself breathing along with him.

A few days after the operation, I was sitting beside

him in the hospital, reading a magazine while he rested. His eyes were shut. All of a sudden, he began moving his hand across the blanket. It seemed like he was searching for something.

"What are you looking for?" I asked.

He patted the blanket. "Your hand."

My chest tightened. Then slowly, fighting a lump in my throat, I slid my hand under his. He gave my fingers a weak squeeze. It was at that moment that I realized something for the first time: He would miss me, too.

Mom went into the kitchen, and I walked upstairs to my dad's office and poked my head in. He was sleeping. Get-well cards sat on the nightstand beside a white poinsettia wrapped in shiny red paper. A crocheted afghan of multicolored granny squares lay across the foot of the bed. Mom took extra care to make sure that his office didn't look like a hospital room. The orange plastic medicine bottles were out of sight. A few pine branches rested on the windowsill. It was the only decorating she had done. Some kids were playing baseball in the park behind our house. I knew Dad would like the sound of that.

Quietly, I walked over to the bed and stood beside him. Nothing was left of his dark and wavy hair. The chemo had taken it. His brow was furrowed, his face lined. His breathing was labored and shallow. It sounded troubled. He reminded me of a baby bird that had fallen out of its nest.

As I stood there, I recalled a time when I was a child and my dad poked his head into my bedroom to see if I was asleep. I wasn't, but I pretended to be. He walked to the bed, leaned over me, then gently stroked my forehead. I could smell his cologne. The memory was one I had long forgotten. I was happy that it came back to me.

After a few moments, I tiptoed out of the room, shut the door, then walked down the hall to my sister's old bedroom. Carol had moved out as soon as she could, but still had some of her things at my parents'. The white bedroom set was hers and the pink chenille bedspread. Most of the books belonged to her, too, including a long row of yellow-spined Nancy Drews, whose image on the covers always reminded me of my sister. Along one entire wall was a large closet with four sliding doors.

"Thanks for helping me with this," Mom said, entering the bedroom.

"You bet."

Mom walked to the closet and slid open one set of doors. Inside were my parents' winter clothes, tablecloths still in their dry cleaning plastic, and my father's old records, mainly a mix of classical, jazz, and recordings of Richard Rodgers's *Victory at Sea*. Dad's leather jacket from his Navy days hung on a hanger. Stitched on the arms and front were large blue and gold patches with emblems of dragons, ships, and eagles' wings. He never wore it after he left the Navy.

Mom kept all her Christmas decorations in the closet. The floor was covered with bags and boxes and plastic tubs. The three-foot space above the shelf was packed with containers labeled "Christmas — Living Room," "Christmas — Kitchen," even "Christmas — Bathroom."

"What do you want me to take down?" I asked, looking up at the shelf.

"All of it," she answered.

I raised an eyebrow. "*All* of it?"

"Yes."

"Well," I said, scratching my head, "if I hurry, we might be finished by New Year's."

"Michael!"

After a chuckle, I clapped my hands together. "OK. Let's get crackin'."

One by one, I started taking the decorations off the shelf and began stacking them on the bed. I pulled down boxes of outdoor lights, a bin of lights for the tree, a tub of bows, a box for stockings, another for garland, and others full of wrapping paper and Christmas cards. Mom had bags of candles, craft supplies, candy canes, pinecones, and still more gift wrap that she'd bought for half off the day after Christmas.

"Why do you save all this stuff?" I asked, rubbing the back of my neck.

Mom didn't answer. She just watched me as I pulled things out. I had no idea how I was going to get it all back up there.

"Be careful with that one," Mom said as I reached for the last box. It held her ornaments.

"Don't worry. I got it."

"Put it here," she said, patting the bedspread.

I placed the box on the bed, flopped into a chair, and looked around the room. "It's a pity we don't have any Christmas decorations," I teased. "We really should get some more."

"You sound just like your dad."

I liked hearing that.

Mom sat down beside the ornament box and examined it. It was nothing fancy — just a large green cardboard box with a red lid bought at Sears many years before. Yellowed masking tape reinforced the corners. After wiping the lid with a dishtowel, Mom removed the tape she'd put on the previous year to hold it down, then opened the box.

There they were — the ornaments — each one carefully wrapped in white tissue paper. Mom took a few of them out of the box and gently pulled away the paper. She smiled at the ornaments as though she were welcoming company that had just arrived. Then she picked one of them up.

Hanging from a hook was a small round bulb — just a bit smaller than a tennis ball — bright pink with three thin silver stripes. The paint was starting to crackle and some of it had chipped off near the top. The words "Merry Christmas," lettered in white, circled the ornament. Mom stared at the bulb, wiped it with her thumb, then held it up for me to see.

"You know when I got this, right?" she asked.

We shared a smile.

"Of course, I do," I said, taking it gently from her hand. "This is where it all began."

Chapter Two - The Bulb

Shirley Johnson graduated from El Dorado High School in 1955. The nearest state college was fifty miles away in Sacramento. But she didn't have a car. Even if she had a way to get there, there was no money for books or tuition. If Shirley wanted to further her education, her only option was to enroll in the Kaiser Foundation School of Nursing in Oakland. In those days, the nursing school was paid for by the hospital. So Shirley moved to the Bay Area. In her suitcase, she carried the items required for entrance to the program: two white dresses, a pair of nurses shoes, two pairs of white stockings, an alarm clock, and a pair of bandage scissors.

In her junior year, Shirley and some of the other nursing students were sent to the VA hospital in Menlo Park to work and study for six months in the psychiatric rehabilitation department. They lived in a nurses' residence on Willow Road. It was an old brick building wrapped with creeping fig. Inside, the house was nothing fancy: three bedrooms upstairs, each with two single beds and a bunk, and a small bathroom that twelve student nurses shared. On the ground floor — a living area with a stone fireplace, a kitchen with the only phone in the building, and a bedroom where Mrs. Anderson, the housemother, lived. A retired RN who still wore her nursing pin with pride, Mrs. Anderson kept a close eye on things. Curfew was at 10:00 sharp. At 10:01, she locked the doors. No men were ever allowed past the living room. If, for some reason, a maintenance man had to go upstairs, Mrs. Anderson would ring a bell, and everyone would announce, "Man on floor!"

Shirley was assigned to work the week of Christmas. It would be her first Christmas away from home, and she tried not to think about it. The same was true for several other junior nurses in the house. To cheer themselves up, Shirley and her friends asked Mrs. Anderson if they could throw a Christmas party at the residence. She agreed and even volunteered to make brownies. The nurses invited a few men from the Bachelor Officers Quarters at nearby Moffett Field. Mrs. Anderson would chaperone.

After pooling their money, the girls walked to Montgomery Ward where they bought a small

Christmas tree, a box of lights, icicles, and two boxes of Shiny Brite ornaments. Each box held twelve pink bulbs decorated with snow scenes and holiday greetings. The white price tags on the lids said 39 cents. They also bought food for snacks, eggnog, and ingredients for baking.

Back at the house, Shirley and her friends, most in curlers, filled celery with cream cheese and wrapped dough around cocktail franks to make pigs in a blanket. They mixed potato salad, greased cookie sheets, and licked beaters while Dean Martin, Johnny Mathis, and Mario Lanza sang on the Hi-Fi. After the tree was trimmed and bowls of nuts, potato chips, and dip were set out around the living room, they went upstairs and painted nails, curled eyelashes, and attached nylons to garter belts.

Shirley borrowed a red, full-skirted tulle dress from her best friend, Maureen. The collar was rounded, the sleeves three-quarter length. The wide fabric belt accentuated Shirley's small waist.

"I'm going to kill you," Maureen said, zipping Shirley into the dress.

"Why?"

"Because my dress looks better on *you* than it does on me!"

Smiling, Shirley put her hands on her hips and

made a spin. "Too tight?"

"No. It's perfect," Maureen replied, sliding on a bracelet. "And you're *not* keeping it."

They laughed together.

Then Maureen set two pairs of shoes on the floor in front of her. "Which ones?" Shirley pointed to the pair of black, open-toed sling-backs. "I agree," said Maureen, sliding them on.

After checking one another's skirts to make sure their ruffled crinolines didn't show (Shirley had starched hers so it wouldn't go flat as easily) and dabbing their necks with Evening in Paris, the two left the room. As they flounced down the staircase, their skirts made swishing sounds, which Shirley found ridiculously satisfying.

The Navy boys arrived just before 7:00. There were five of them. When they walked in, Shirley was sitting on the piano bench in front of a black baby grand. It belonged to Mrs. Anderson, who normally kept the top down to keep the dust out, but put it up for the party. Just beside the piano stood the Christmas tree. The lights were on. The room was warm from the fire in the fireplace.

Shirley immediately spotted a young officer with dark wavy hair as he took off his leather jacket and placed it on the coat stand. He wore a blue sweater. Shirley thought he looked handsome.

When the officer entered the room, he glanced in her direction, and their eyes met. Since Shirley was seated at the piano, he assumed she was a musician. The officer came from a family of musicians. As he crossed the floor toward her, Shirley pretended to be straightening her skirt while making a little more room on the bench.

"Hi," he said, flashing a broad smile. "My name's Tom."

Shirley noticed that his skin was fresh from shaving. The cleft in his chin reminded her of Cary Grant's. "I'm Shirley."

"You know the best place to listen to a grand piano?" Tom asked, still smiling.

"No," she said, waiting for something funny. "Where?"

"Underneath. You feel like you're in the middle of the music." Shirley smiled. "Ever lie underneath a grand piano while someone is playing?"

"No," she chuckled.

He liked the sound of her laugh.

"You should try it sometime," Tom said. He gestured to the piano bench. "May I?"

"Certainly."

The bench was small for the two of them. He was glad about that.

"Nice dress," he said.

"Thank you."

Then Tom slapped his knees. "I'm stumped," he said. "What kind of flowers does a man buy a woman wearing a red dress?"

Charmed, Shirley played along. "Well, definitely not red. White, for sure."

"What kind?"

"Oh . . . carnations. Or gardenias."

"Which would you want?" he asked, tapping her shoulder with his.

"Mmm . . . gardenias."

Tom's smile accentuated the twinkle in his eye. "Next time you wear that dress, I'll have to remember that."

Together the two talked and laughed and got to know each other. He discovered that Shirley had just turned twenty, was the oldest of six kids, liked Chinese food, loved the movies, and had one more year to go in nursing school. She learned that Tom was a lieutenant junior grade, was twenty-four years old, had no brothers or sisters, was originally from Chicago, followed the stock market, and had beautiful blue eyes that she tried very hard not to stare at.

Suddenly, Maureen clapped her hands and announced that it was time to sing. She scooted Tom and Shirley off the bench and sat down to play. As the group gathered around the piano, Tom stood behind Shirley. Someone passed out carol books, and Maureen started playing the introduction to "The First Noel."

"I love this one," Tom said. As an excuse to stand closer to Shirley, he leaned over her shoulder and squinted at the music. Then he gave her a grin. "Hard to read such small print."

Soon everyone started singing. Tom sang the bass line, sometimes tenor. He never did look at the music; he knew all the words already. What a lovely voice he had, Shirley thought. In the middle of "O Come, All Ye Faithful," she stopped singing just to listen to him.

"You lost?" Tom asked Shirley in the middle of the song.

A blush crept up her face. "Yes," she heard herself say. She looked down, her lips pressed into a smile. "I guess I am."

But Tom didn't hear her. By then he was already singing again. He was having such a good time.

As the group sang carol after carol, Shirley lost her place a few more times, and Tom's eyesight grew worse and worse. By the time Maureen played "Silent Night" on the last page, Tom's arm was around Shirley's shoulder. She welcomed it.

After the last verse, everyone applauded. Tom dropped his arm as Shirley turned to him. "You know," she said with a smirk, "this would have sounded *so* much better if we'd all been under the piano." Tom threw his head back and laughed.

As the others stepped away, Shirley and Tom lingered on the bench.

"So," Shirley asked, "what do you enjoy most about Christmas?"

Tom pursed his lips and thought about it for a moment. ". . . The smells."

Shirley smiled. "Which ones?"

Tom liked this game. "Mmm . . . turkey in the oven . . . the scent of pine sap on your hands after you cut down the tree . . . a wood-burning fire. And . . ." He rubbed his chin, pretending to think hard. "Canned pumpkin."

"Canned *pumpkin*?"

He tried to sound serious. "Yeah."

Shirley pushed him with her shoulder. "You do not."

Tom grinned as she laughed. He had tried to make her.

"And you?" Tom asked. "What do *you* like best?"

"Well . . ." she answered with a smile, "I like walking into a department store and discovering that they've just put out their Christmas decorations." She paused. "And . . . I love reading cookie recipes.

Aaaand . . . oh, yes! I like seeing the first tree of the season tied to the top of a car. *That's* when Christmas begins for me."

Tom's face broke into a wide grin. Then, looking at the tree, he got an idea. He stood up, stepped over to it, and removed one of the pink bulbs. On it were the words "Merry Christmas." He returned to Shirley and sat back down. "This is for you," he said, handing her the ornament, "to remember our first Christmas together." His eyes were smiling.

After a while, Tom noticed Mrs. Anderson glance at her watch. It was 9:45, almost time for the men to leave. Tom jumped up, winked at Shirley, and gave her hand a squeeze. Then he grabbed his buddies and headed toward the door. Shirley and the other girls followed. Coats and hats were put on, hands were shaken, and good-byes were said. And the men were gone.

After the food was put away, the candles blown out, and the porch light turned off, Shirley walked up to her bedroom with her gift from Tom. She smiled at it as she climbed the stairs. The room was dark. Two of her roommates were already asleep. Shirley set the bulb on her nightstand, then quietly got out of her dress and hung it on the closet door. After putting on her pajamas, she crawled into bed. From her pillow, she looked over at the ornament. A wedge of moonlight spilling through a crack in the curtains caught its light. Smiling softly, Shirley replayed the evening in her mind. She fell asleep thinking of how nice Tom looked in blue.

Chapter Three

Mom wrapped the pink ornament back in tissue paper, set the lid on the box, and surveyed the room. "It's a lot to carry." Then she turned and looked at me. "Would you like a grilled cheese sandwich?"

"Sure," I said, standing up. "That sounds good."

"I'll make you one while you bring all this down." Mom got up from the bed and started to leave. "Now be careful with it."

"Mom!"

"Well, I have to say that. That's what moms say, isn't it?" And she left the room. I was happy to see her smile.

As I carried everything down the stairs and passed my dad's office, I thought about my father. I pictured him flirting with my mom at that Christmas party. I knew he was a charmer. My girlfriends in high school used to come over to my house just to see him. They thought he was cute. I imagined him standing in his leather jacket on the deck of an aircraft carrier as it sailed across the Pacific. I remembered a story my mother told me about her sneaking in the window of the nurse's residence and tiptoeing past Mrs. Anderson's room on a night when Dad's ball team won and they stayed out late to celebrate. I thought about him not being able to come down for Christmas Eve dinner.

After my fifth trip downstairs, all the decorations were finally in the living room. The couch, coffee table, and the top of the stereo cabinet were covered with boxes and bags. As I set the ornament box on the dining room table, Mom came into the room and said my sandwich was ready.

I joined her in the kitchen, where two pumpkin pies were cooling on a cutting board. Beside it — a red-handled rolling pin, aluminum cookie cutters shaped like bells, reindeer, and snowmen, and a green metal recipe box stuffed with yellowed newspaper clippings and grease-stained index cards with hand-written recipes. The turkey was in the oven. The room smelled like Christmas.

Taking a seat, I spotted three large poinsettias sitting in the sink. They looked like they were in pretty bad shape.

"Did you forget to water your flowers?" I asked.

"No. I'm hoping to save them. The guy at Home Depot was throwing them away." She walked over to one of the plants and started picking off the dead leaves.

My smile widened. "Did you crawl into the dumpster to rescue them?"

"No!" she cried, pretending to be offended. "They were *beside* the dumpster."

"Ha!" I hooted. "Saved by the Poinsettia Fairy."

Mom loved her flowers. Near the sink, a Christmas cactus exploded with red. On the counter, purple African violets sat on Blue Willow saucers, and a lone amaryllis looked like it was just waking up for the holiday. If my mom spotted a new bloom on her morning glories just outside the kitchen window, and my father was nearby, she would pull him over to show him. My mother was known to name her plants and even pray for them. No doubt, she'd already prayed over the poinsettias in the sink. From the sliding glass door, I could see out to the patio where chrysanthemums, cyclamen, pansies, and ivy tumbled out of large terracotta pots. Since my father's diagnosis, Mom spent more time in her garden. She wanted my dad to see lots of flowers.

Mom brought over a sandwich and a glass of orange juice and set them in front of me on a red placemat. The sandwich was cut into four triangles, the way she'd always cut my sandwiches since I was a kid. Then she poured herself a cup of tea and sat down across from me.

"How's Karen?" she asked, bobbing the teabag in her cup.

"Fine. She's still decorating the house."

"I thought she was finished."

I made a face. "She found an empty wall."

Mom gave a thin smile then looked down and smoothed out her apron. It wasn't wrinkled.

I set my sandwich down and looked at her. "Are you OK?"

She nodded, close-mouthed. I knew that look. If she'd spoken, she would have started to cry.

I tried to cheer her up. "You know what Karen and Christopher were doing when I left?" I paused one beat. "Setting reindeer food on the front porch."

Mom looked surprised.

I leaned toward her and grinned. "Do you know how to make reindeer food?"

She shook her head.

"Well, I just learned. You mix up oatmeal and glitter."

"*Glitter?*"

"Yes."

"Why?" She was smiling.

"Well, apparently, when Rudolph flies overhead, his shiny nose reflects in it and makes it sparkle so he can spot the food."

Mom laughed. Mission accomplished.

When Dad was diagnosed, my mother jumped into nurse mode. She was a caretaker. Mom nursed her own father at the end of his life and took Dad's mother in after her first heart attack. My mom's whole life was dedicated to taking care of people. For my father, she cooked special meals and researched alternative therapies. She washed him, shaved him, and dressed him in his baseball jerseys when his teammates came over to visit. I admired the way she still managed to put together Christmas dinner through all this. I didn't know how she was able to do it. If Karen were ill, I couldn't have done what my mom did. I couldn't have kept going.

Mom said it was her faith that kept her strong. As long as I could remember, every morning my mother would sit in the living room to pray and read her King James Bible. (She didn't believe in those "new-fangled" ones.) "Daily reading of God's word brings nourishment to the soul," she always said. "Like adding blueberries to muffins."

Mom's Bible sat in the center of the coffee table next to the candy dish. The leather binding was falling off from years of opening and closing it. Inside, passages were highlighted and the margins were filled with notes. One morning, when she was talking with God about something, I tiptoed past her on my way to the kitchen. She looked up with her eyes still closed and said, "We're out of milk. Have toast," and went right back to her prayer.

But Mom didn't just know the Good Book. She lived it. Her potholders were worn from pulling casseroles out of the oven for those in need, and the handle on her aluminum cake carrier was barely hanging on, too. Her choir folder at church was coming apart at the edges. She worked at rummage sales to raise money for missionaries she'd never met and arranged flowers for the Sunday pulpit (and was secretly delighted when the pastor told her that last Easter the church was packed because of *her* hydrangeas). Mom visited the veterans on her days off from the VA hospital, where she still worked part-time. More than once she sneaked candy bars in for her patients.

Before Dad became ill, Mom attended church twice a week, sometimes three. When we were kids, she would bribe us with candy to sit still in the pews and not play with the communion glasses or the offering basket when they came down the row. She didn't take well to church bulletins being turned into paper airplanes. In Sunday school, we dared not horse around. Mom was the teacher.

My dad only went to church twice a year, on Easter and Christmas. Both days, he got up early and drove to church by himself. He was back home before we were up. Most Sunday mornings, he'd work in his office, or sit on the couch and watch a game or read the paper. This was always difficult for my mother. She never accepted it.

I remember many a Sunday morning when Mom asked my dad to join us, and he said no. She would say something about raising the children properly. Dad would tell her to stop preaching, and we'd leave without him. On these mornings, Carol and I would sit quietly in the back seat of the car. Sometimes my mom cried. Once, when she was pulling out of the driveway, Mom looked over her shoulder and snapped, "Your father *is* a believer. *Don't* be thinking he's not." My sister and I were silent. "Sometimes things happen to us that make people not want to go to church."

I set my napkin down and scooted my chair from under the table.

"That was great," I said, standing up.

"Would you like another one?" Mom asked.

I grabbed my belt and tugged at it. "I'd love one, but I better not. I didn't ask Santa for a new pair of pants."

Stepping into the living room, I found the bin labeled "Tree Lights" by the coffee table and smiled when I took off the lid. It was packed full, each strand neatly tied with bread bag twisties.

"Who needs five hundred yards of lights?" I hollered.

Mom called out from the kitchen. "Your father."

It was true. My dad loved Christmas. There was something about the holiday that brought out the best in him. Every December he hung more outside lights than anyone else on the street. He whistled carols around the house, kept Christmas albums playing on the stereo, and stopped by the bakery to buy animals made of marzipan and German *stollen* filled with candied fruit.

Actually, Mom claimed that Dad married her for Christmas. A year after they met, my dad spent the holiday with my mom's family. They weren't married yet. My father had never experienced anything like it. On Christmas morning, presents tied with curly ribbon and stick-on bows covered the living room carpet. Opening gifts was a flurry of tearing paper, smiling for the camera, and searching for the next package with your name on it. When it was time to sit down to dinner, nine people squeezed in around the table on four kitchen chairs, two folding ones, a piano bench with a wobbly leg, and one stool topped with a phonebook, then talked and joked and laughed and sneaked food to the dog and cleaned up spilled milk. Dad loved the bustle and commotion and noise of it all. Up till then, Christmas for him had been a lonely time. After his father was killed in the war, it was just him and his mother. With my mom, Dad found the Christmas he was always looking for.

Christmas is my favorite time of year, too. I like watching *It's a Wonderful Life* and reciting lines along with Jimmy Stewart. I enjoy arriving a little late to church and hearing choir anthems pour out of it like a giant music box. I get a kick out of driving down streets with lots of Christmas lights and guessing what their electric bills must be. I like turning off the lights at home after Karen has gone to bed and sitting in the dark, staring at the lighted tree. One year, I took Christopher out of bed while he was asleep and placed him under the tree so that he'd wake up under it. I'm sure the main reason I love Christmas, though, is that it was the time of year when I felt closest to my father.

Growing up, my dad and I used to drive our Ford station wagon to Joe's Tree Farm up in the foothills and cut down our tree. It was the one thing we did together every year. We always had a real tree. My dad would never think of getting an artificial one. Back then Joe Sr. still worked on the tree lot. At the farm, as soon as my Dad and I would step out of the car, we'd be enveloped by the smell of evergreen. All around us rows and rows of trees stood like marching bands in the Macy's parade. Dad knew all about picking Christmas trees. Spruce trees, he said, drop their needles too easily. White pines don't hold heavy ornaments well, but Douglas firs hold up indoors *and* they smell good, too. Dad always bought a Douglas.

According to Joe Jr., there are two kinds of tree-shoppers — those who take the first one they see, and those who need to look at every single tree on the lot at least once before they decide. My father was in the second group. He could take hours searching for just the right one. When he finally found the tree he wanted, he'd walk around it about five times, examining the branches and sniffing the needles. Then he'd circle it another five times to make sure it was full enough and tall enough and shaped well enough for the living room.

When I was very young, I would ask Dad if *I* could cut down the tree, but he'd say no, of course. The saw was too dangerous. When I got a little older, he would let me hold the handle of the saw as he kept his hand on mine. After a while, I would get tired, and he'd finish the job alone. Some years later, after he cut the tree down, he would let me saw off some of the smaller branches while he watched. Finally, when I was twelve, he handed me the saw and let me cut the whole tree myself. I felt like a man.

As soon as we'd get the tree home, Dad would saw the trunk again, then put it in a pail of water on the side of the house. After it soaked a couple of days, he'd set out newspapers on the living room floor, then place the red and green metal Christmas tree stand on the paper. Mom would hold the tree in place while Dad lay on the floor, tightening the screws into the trunk and filling the stand with water. After he crawled out, my folks would agree that their new tree was better than last year's.

I took the lights out, stretched them across the living room floor, and attached the ends to one another until I had one long giant strand. After double-checking all the connections, I plugged them in. I was happy they all lit. (It's always a relief the moment you first plug in your Christmas tree lights that have been hibernating the whole year and discover that they still work.) Then I started wrapping the lights around the tree.

In our house, all tree lights *had* to be white. Blinking lights were not allowed. When I was around seven or eight, I asked if we could have flashing colored lights like the neighbor across the street, and my dad looked at me as though I had just asked him if I could start smoking. Once, by accident, he bought a strand of blinking lights and spent an hour trying to find that one light in a thousand that was causing all the others to blink. When he finally found it, he shouted, "Ah ha!" then opened the door and threw it outside into the bushes like it was a nasty old spider.

While I worked on the lights, Mom sat at the dining room table, unwrapping the ornaments from their tissue paper. Her face was locked in a smile as she inspected each one, wiped it off, put on a hook, and set it on the table. There were old ornaments, new ones, and those made at school. My mother could not throw an ornament away. She saved every walnut with bauble eyes, pipe cleaner reindeer, and Styrofoam ball stuck with pins and beads. If an ornament was cracked or broken, she hung it on the tree anyway with the damaged part facing the trunk. When hanging ornaments, Mom was known to talk to them: "Nope, you're too heavy there." "Let's find you a better branch." "Well, I can't see you all the way down there!"

Mom turned to me, holding a baby food jar. "Remember this one?"

I cracked a smile. "Second Grade. Mrs. Watson."

The jar was empty. The tag wrapped around the

lid said, "Contents — Christmas Spirit from 1968. Do Not Open."

"She was a brave one," I said, chuckling. "I remember the whole class was running around the room with those baby food jars, scooping up the air and sealing them as fast as we could with our lids." I laughed. "Of course, we were *sure* that we hadn't captured enough Christmas spirit, so we'd take the lids off and run around some more."

Mom shook her head. "God bless Mrs. Watson."

After I finished hanging the lights and wrapping the garland around the tree, it was time to start putting on the ornaments. Mom had trained us in ornament hanging: The heaviest ones go on the bottom, the smallest on top. Never hang a large ornament on a small branch, or it will sag. Don't put your ornaments too close together; they need room to breathe. Remember to place them inside the tree, not just on the end of the branches. Ugly ones go in the back. And hang your nicest ornaments in the best spots — at eye-level on the side closest to the door, so that when someone walks into the house, it's the first thing they see.

Even when all the ornaments were on the tree, my mom was never completely finished trimming it. She liked to stretch out her decorating. As branches drooped, she'd adjust the garland and move the ornaments around. Like a mother who always makes sure that her child is properly dressed, my mom couldn't pass the tree without checking on it.

Mom picked up the pink bulb then handed it to me. It was tradition to hang that one first. The ornament's ridged aluminum cap wasn't shiny anymore. The metal hook was tarnished.

"Put this near the top," she instructed.

I looked at her sideways. "Mom."

Her mouth rose into a smile as I placed it on the tree. Next, she handed me a wooden heart about the size of my hand. Attached to the front was the plaster topper from my parents' wedding cake. Standing arm in arm, the groom wore a white dinner jacket, the bride — a lace skirt that was glued around her waist. Under her veil, she had long dark hair like my mom used to have. As a child, I thought that the person who made the bride knew my mother and fashioned it after her. A few weeks after their wedding, Dad had taken a piece of scrap wood and cut it into the shape of a heart. He carved a design around the edges, sanded it smooth, and stained it. Then he attached the bride and groom. On the back of the heart he wrote, "Thanks for loving me."

After I hung the heart, Mom handed me the next

ornament. It was a baby rattle. The writing on its surface was almost all rubbed off now. Smiling, I held it up to my ear and gave it a shake. "It still works."

As I walked around the tree searching for a place to hang it, I spotted my parents' wedding photo on top of the piano. In it, my dad, mom, and father's mother stood on the altar steps, framed by two white candle stands. It was the only photo I had ever seen from that day. As I looked at the photograph, I remembered as a kid asking my mom why *her* parents weren't in the picture. She said they hadn't attended. When I asked why, Mom told me to go wash my hands for dinner.

Chapter Four - The Rattle

It was a simple wedding. Tom's mother, Mathilda, flew out from Chicago to attend. It was her first plane ride. The wedding took place on a November evening in 1959 at Willow Glen Methodist Church.

Tom wore his dress blues. The jacket was double-breasted with two gold stripes and one star on each cuff. Shirley looked radiant in a lace-covered taffeta gown that she bought the week before at Hales department store. The dress had a fitted bodice and a ballerina-length skirt. A row of covered buttons ran up the sleeves. The store threw in a garter and gave her *Betty Crocker's Picture Cookbook* as a gift. Shirley made the tulle veil herself. She'd tried to copy the one Audrey Hepburn wore in *Funny Face*.

Tom's friend Steve stood as best man. Maureen, dressed in emerald green, was Shirley's maid of honor. Both women held small bouquets of white roses that Maureen put together with nursery tape the night before. Mathilda sat in the front row wearing a purple satin dress, a beaded pillbox hat, and a voluminous orchid corsage that everyone had to be careful not to squish when giving her a hug.

When the organist began playing "Ave Maria," Shirley walked alone down the aisle. Her mom and dad were not there. They'd sent Shirley's two younger brothers, fifteen- and eighteen-years-old, to represent the family. Each wore a borrowed sport coat and a narrow bow tie. After the vows were exchanged, Shirley looked out at her brothers and cried behind her veil.

At the end of the ceremony, when the organist played Wagner and cameras flashed, the newlyweds ran out of the church through a rain of rice. The guests met at Maureen's parents' apartment for a small reception, where Maureen's mother served punch made with orange sherbet and ginger ale. Shirley's nursing friends handed out favors of candied almonds that they'd wrapped in white netting. After the toast, Tom and Shirley cut the cake — two tiers topped with white icing and aluminum flowers. The plaster bride and groom sat on top. Maureen caught the bouquet; Shirley threw it to her on purpose. For her going-away outfit, Shirley changed into a full-skirted black dress with a sweetheart neckline, black gloves, and the pearls

Tom had given her. Before the newlyweds left, Tom's Navy buddies sneaked away and filled their bed with corn flakes.

Six months later, and after Tom's last naval tour to Korea, the young couple moved to Chicago. Tom's commission in the Navy was over. He had gotten a job with a major tax firm. The two drove cross-country in Tom's '52 blue De Soto sedan. Packed with suitcases, a tent with wooden poles, a Coleman lantern, and a green double-burner stove, they camped along the way.

Tom and Shirley stayed with Tom's mother for a few weeks until they found their own apartment on the top floor of an old brick four-story walk-up with corner bay windows and a fire escape in the back. The tiles in the bathroom were pink. The Frigidaire was turquoise. Their rent was ninety dollars a month. The stairs in the building weren't fun to climb every day, especially if they got to the ground floor and realized that they forgot the umbrella, but Shirley said the trek was good for her legs, and both were grateful that they didn't have a dog that had to be let out three times a day, like their neighbor's.

Almost exactly a year after they were married, Shirley gave birth to a son. They named him Michael after Shirley's father. Michael was a month early. He weighed only five-and-a-half pounds and had to stay in the hospital for over a week before they could take him home. Soon after Michael was born, Tom and Shirley decided that Tom should get his Masters in Business Administration, so he left the tax firm to go to school. When Michael was three months old, Shirley went back to work full-time at a hospital across town to support the family.

The work was hard, especially when she had to lift patients, and the hours were long. Oftentimes, Shirley would take the night shift so that Tom could watch Michael and they wouldn't have to pay a babysitter. After work, she'd still have to wash her uniform in the sink, polish her shoes till they looked new out of the box, and clean and starch her white nurse's cap before folding it into a "flying bedpan" shape to dry.

Life wasn't easy those first few years in Chicago. Tom and Shirley owned four pieces of furniture: a sofa bed, a crib, a high chair, and a chrome table with a red formica top that Shirley bought for three dollars from a neighbor who was moving. In the winter, when the heat in the building went off at eleven o'clock and ice would form on the inside of the windows, Shirley would turn on the oven and lay Michael on the kitchen counter so he'd be warm. His smelly diapers froze overnight in the pail out on the balcony, and

Shirley would have to let them thaw before washing them in the bathtub.

One evening, when Shirley was at home writing Christmas cards (She enjoyed signing them from "Tom and Shirley" and not just "Shirley") there was a knock at the door. Who could that be? Shirley thought. She wasn't expecting anyone.

Shirley got up and leaned against the door. "Who is it?"

"It's me, dear — Mathilda."

"Oh!"

Shirley unlocked the door, and there stood Tom's mother.

"Hello, dear!" Mathilda cried, slightly out of breath. She was bundled in a long navy blue coat with large round buttons. A Christmas tree brooch with red and green glass stones was pinned to her fox fur collar. Two clip-on earrings, also shaped like trees, completed the set. A feathered hat with netting and pearls sat askew on her head from the climb upstairs. Her powdered face and white hair, which she liked to call the color of champagne, set off her bright red lipstick.

"Hello," said Shirley. "What a surprise."

Behind Mathilda stood two teenage boys. One held a Christmas tree in a metal stand. The other carried a mahogany rocking chair. The two teenagers followed

Mathilda as she flew inside and scanned the room. Her wisteria perfume trailed behind her. "Put it in the corner," Mathilda said to the young man holding the tree. "Be careful. And you . . ." she said, pointing to the lad with the rocking chair. "Set that next to the couch. No. A little closer. Careful. No. A little more. Yes, that's right. Good." Her silver bracelets accentuated each gesture like downbeats in a waltz. As she directed the scene, a wisp of blue feather flew off her hat and floated in the air.

Shirley said nothing. Her mind was on the mess of baby toys on the floor and the pin curls under her scarf. She was relieved that the laundry drying in the back room was out of sight. Finally, Mathilda gave each of her helpers a quarter and sent them on their way.

"You'll *never* guess what happened," Mathilda said, flopping herself into the rocking chair with her coat still on. "I was at the corner lot today and accidentally bought *two* Christmas trees! Silly me." She set down her red handbag and began removing her matching leather gloves. "And when I went to return one, they wouldn't take it back." Mathilda slapped her knees. "Well! I can't possibly fit *two* trees in my house. Please won't you and Tommy take one?"

Shirley sat down across from her and smiled at the tree.

"And I thought you might like to have this old rocking chair, too," Mathilda continued, giving it a good push. "I used to rock Tommy in it. Did you know that?" The wood made a loud creak. "I'm afraid it's rather noisy. Nothing some use won't cure." Mathilda sighed; it almost sounded like singing. "I don't use it anymore now that I've got my recliner." She patted the arms and made a sad face. "Poor thing. Rocking chairs should be sat in, you know. Too much time without company isn't good for them. Just like a piano." Mathilda liked to use this comparison. She was a piano teacher, had been all her life, and always talked about pianos as though they were alive.

"Thank you," Shirley said. "We'd love to have it." She looked at the tree. "And the tree is beautiful. Thank you very much."

"My pleasure." Mathida glanced at her watch. "When's that husband of yours coming home?"

"Oh, not for a while. He's out late tonight." Shirley stood up quickly. "Where are my manners? Would you like something to drink? Some tea?"

"Oh, no, no, no," Mathilda said, standing up. "I must be going, dear. I haven't finished my shopping yet." Shirley was secretly relieved. She had tea, but nothing to serve with it. And her teacups didn't match.

Mathilda walked to the crib in the corner of the room and leaned over it. Michael was sleeping with a yellow pacifier in his mouth. His grandmother gently stroked his head and moved a squeeze toy closer to his hands. Then she turned, swooped up her handbag and gloves, and stepped toward the door, where she checked herself in the mirror, adjusted her hat, and gave an approving smile.

"Now, dear," Mathilda said, turning to Shirley, "make *sure* you water that tree every day." She presented her cheek for Shirley to kiss. "Good-bye. Give my love to Tom."

Shirley opened the door, and Mathilda started down the stairs. One flight below, she stopped and looked up. "And, dear, make sure you keep it away from the radiator! That would be the *death* of it."

"Oh, yes," Shirley called down. "We will. Thanks again. Good-bye."

Shirley listened to Mathilda's heels echo through the stairwell before stepping back into the apartment. When she closed the door, the scent of wisteria lingered in the room. Then, Shirley filled the tree stand with water as she'd been told and wrapped one of Michael's baby blankets around the base. She fetched a box from the closet that held the few ornaments she had and hung them on the tree. Since she didn't have enough hooks, she used paperclips. While covering a paper plate star with aluminum foil, Shirley smiled thinking about how surprised Tom would be when he saw their new tree.

That first Christmas in Chicago, Tom and Shirley decided that they would not buy each other presents. They just didn't have the money. But Tom wanted to give something to Shirley. Plus, this was his son's first Christmas, and he wanted to celebrate it.

So, one night while Shirley was at work, Tom went to the coat closet and opened the door. He pulled the string for the light bulb, pushed the coats aside, and searched through boxes of old yearbooks, papers, and textbooks that cost too much to throw away. Finally, he found what he was looking for and carried it to the kitchen table. It was a white shoebox. He hadn't opened it for years. Tom stared at it a moment before jiggling off the lid.

Inside lay a cloth diaper with two pins and a little white T-shirt. Of course, he didn't remember wearing them. He was only nine months old at the time. He had no recollection of the day Mathilda and his father, Cyril, visited the orphanage on the outskirts of Chicago and walked down the rows of white iron cribs, lined up like cots in an Army barracks, looking for a baby. In Tom's room alone there were over twenty children. And, of course, he didn't recall the moment when the couple stopped at his crib, and he beamed at them, and Mathilda instantly fell in love with his brilliant blue eyes.

In those days, one could "try out" a baby. When Mathilda brought Tommy home for the weekend, her mother said that he looked sickly, was too small, and would give her trouble. Mathilda adored the child immediately and wanted to keep him, but her mother insisted that it was a bad idea. Reluctantly, Mathilda returned him. But for days, she couldn't stop thinking of that little boy. She couldn't get his angelic face out of her mind. A week later, against her mother's wishes, Mathilda and Cyril went back to the orphanage and adopted him.

Tom lifted the T-shirt out of the box and read the note pinned to the front. It was in Mathilda's handwriting:

> *This is the shirt that Tommy wore when we brought him home from the orphanage. It was all he had.*

The box held other things that Tom had saved — report cards, swimming medals, old baseball cards. There was a bag of marbles and a small stuffed lamb. Tom pulled out the lamb and held it up. It was off-white with dark glass eyes and floppy ears. Patches of the lamb's coat were threadbare. On one of the ears, attached by a round metal button, was a yellow fabric tag with the word *Steiff*. As Tom stared at its face, an image pushed itself to the front of his mind. Instantly, he was somewhere else, standing over a crib. Shutting his eyes, he tried to hug the thought.

After a few moments, Tom set the lamb back into the box. Then he spotted what he was looking for. It was a rattle — light blue, about four inches long, and made of plastic. The handle was shaped like a rocking horse. On the ball was a smiling face with blue eyes just like his. Tom shook the rattle and smiled. Then he grabbed a black pen from the counter. On the back of the ball he wrote "Merry Christmas, Sug." That's what he always called Shirley. It wasn't easy to write on the surface, so he went over it again. Next, he took a yellow diaper pin and stuck it through the hole at the end of the handle. The head of the pin was shaped like a duck. When he was finished, Tom hung it on the side of the tree facing the front door. It wasn't much, but he was happy with his ornament.

When Shirley got home from work just after midnight, the radio was on, Tom was sound asleep on the sofa bed with a textbook by his side, and Michael was sleeping in his crib. The scent of the tree filled the apartment; Shirley loved the smell. She fixed

Michael's blanket, then walked over to Tom and tucked him in, too. After getting ready for bed, she turned out the light and crawled in beside her husband. As she lay there, she chuckled to herself thinking about Mathilda pretending to buy two trees by accident. Soon, Shirley fell asleep. She would discover her new ornament in the morning.

Chapter Five

I hung the rattle on the tree close to the piano. The diaper pin was still hooked on the handle. I heard the story of the rattle from my mom, not my dad. In fact, pretty much everything I knew about my father's past I'd learned from my mother or my grandmother.

Mom was the one who told me that my father used to sing. He and three Navy buddies sang a Calypso number at a talent show, won first prize, and almost appeared on *The Ed Sullivan Show*. It was from my mom that I found out Dad used to work with wood, that he bought her wedding ring set for $399 on an installment plan, and that once he tried out for the Chicago Bears. Dad never told me any of these things.

Mom informed me that Dad's father, Cyril, had been killed in the war when my father was just a boy. Dad never talked about it. Mom also revealed that he never liked being an only child; he wished he had brothers and sisters. When I asked my mom if Dad ever spoke about being adopted, she said that she asked him a couple of times, but he never wanted to discuss it.

My father was a mystery to me, a book that wouldn't open its pages. Though I asked him several times, he never got around to pulling out the slides from his tours on the aircraft carrier. When I asked him where he proposed to Mom, he wouldn't give me a serious answer. He said in a peanut butter factory.

One day at my parents' house, I came across a box of old black-and-white photos of him. I pored over them, studying their details. In one photograph, he was playing football. In another, he was fishing with a friend. In a third, he was sitting with a buddy, their arms around one another's shoulders and huge smiles on their faces. I wanted to be in the picture with them. I swiped the photo.

Growing up, I soaked up every detail of my father's life. I knew all his spots — where he set his keys, his trench coat, his shoes, his eyeglasses. I knew where he kept his tools and where he dropped his change after he got home from work. I knew that one of the clasps was broken on his black leather briefcase, what tie he wore most often, and that the indentation in his can of black Kiwi shoe polish was deeper than in the brown. I knew what part of the lawn he started on when he mowed it, and that seven rubber bands on his office door handle meant he had read seven newspapers that week. I knew that he crossed his *t*s above the letter and that he didn't close his *g*s all the way. I made my *g*s like his.

Once, when I was ten, I walked into his bedroom when he wasn't home and looked through his dresser. In the bottom drawer, I found gloves and epaulets from his Navy days. Before I pulled them out, I made sure to remember exactly where each lay so I could return them to their correct spots. I discovered a baseball jersey, his swimming trunks, and a cashmere scarf from Marshall Field's. I pulled out unworn dress shirts still wrapped in their plastic and a wallet that had never been used. In another drawer, I found sock rolls, belts, handkerchiefs, and a money clip engraved with his initials. I picked up a pair of silver and black cufflinks and remembered watching him trying to insert one through the hole in his cuff, then finally giving up and calling my mom for help. As I put the cufflinks back, I could picture him pulling his suit jacket on and giving each shirt cuff a yank so they'd pop out like bread in a toaster. In the same drawer, I found a bundle of Father's Day cards and valentines made out of red construction paper and white paper doilies. There were letters to Santa and even an envelope labeled "Michael's Tooth." I was happy to find these things.

It wasn't just his dresser I went through. I also searched through his desk and medicine cabinet. I counted the hotel soaps he collected when he went on business trips. I took the gray plastic stopper off his bottle of Old Spice and stung my cheeks when I slapped it on my face. Going through his things, I felt vaguely sad. Somewhere in my young heart, I sensed that this was not how a son should get to know his father.

One weekend, when I was home from college, Dad and I were sitting alone in the living room. He was reading the paper and drinking a beer. It was silent. I thought — if I want to know this man, I need to ask him questions; he isn't going to volunteer anything. After taking a deep breath, I looked straight at him and said, "Dad, what's your greatest dream?" It felt awkward; I'd never asked him anything personal like this before. He looked up from the paper and stared hard at me, like a chess player deciding on his next move. He was thinking, but not about the answer. I could see by his expression. He knew what he wanted to say; he was thinking about whether or not he should tell me. There was a heavy silence, then finally he made some comment about hoping the Raiders won their next game and went back to reading the sports page.

Now that he was ill, there were so many questions I wanted to ask him — about his childhood, his friends, his pets, his jobs, his loves, his faith. In what ways did I remind him of himself? Was there anything he regretted not asking his parents? What was he most grateful for? Was he scared to die? But I couldn't bring myself to ask him anything. I was too afraid — fearful of it being awkward, worried that he'd give me another flippant answer, or that he wouldn't answer at all.

Mom glanced at her watch. "I'd better go check on your father."

"Is he awake?" I asked.

"I think so. It's just about time for him to take his medicine." Mom went into the kitchen, poured Dad a glass of juice, then started up the stairs. "I'll be right down," she called.

"I'll go with you," I said, following her.

Upstairs, Mom tapped on the door then entered the office. Together, we walked into the room. Dad was awake now. He smiled when he saw me.

"Michael," he said, softly.

"Hi, Dad."

I stepped over to his bed.

"What a nice shirt," he said.

I let out a laugh. Dad always said that. Then I sat in the chair beside the bed and watched while Mom helped him sit up. I noticed that his pajama shirt was too big on him now.

"How are you doing?" I asked.

"Oh, couldn't kill a weed."

The words made me smile. He always said that, too.

As Mom adjusted his pillows, I looked around the room. I hadn't spent a lot of time there. As a child, his office was off limits. On two walls hung shelves full of trophies, baseball caps, and team photos. Propped up on one shelf was a book Carol made for him one year for his birthday. It was titled *Dad's Favorite Sayings*. It included his most famous phrases like: "You deserve a D for common sense, but you get your allowance anyway" and "Go ask your mother."

On his desk sat his adding machine, a small CD player, and a wooden box where he kept his pencils and pens. Tacked on the wall was a calendar, a crayon drawing from Christopher with "I Love Papa!" written on it, and a photo of my mom. It was probably taken when she was around thirty. She was standing on the beach wearing a large floppy hat, white sunglasses, and a blue two-piece bathing suit — my Dad's favorite.

Spread out neatly across the top of his desk lay bills and envelopes. The envelopes were stamped, the checkbook open. A ballpoint pen sat beside it pointing to the last entry. When I realized why these things were there, I inhaled sharply. Dad had set out all the bills for my mom, preparing everything for her in case he was no longer there to pay them.

"I better check on dinner," Mom said, setting the glass on the nightstand. "You stay and visit." And she left the room.

For a moment it was silent. I wasn't sure what to say. Then, spotting the CD player, I asked if he'd like to listen to some music, and he said yes. I picked up three CDs and smiled at him. "Do you want Heifetz, Heifetz, or . . . Heifetz?"

Dad smiled back. He only had three CDs to his name: Jascha Heifetz playing the *Mendelssohn Violin Concerto*, Heifetz performing the *Tchaikovsky Violin Concerto*, and the *Beethoven Violin Concerto*, played by Heifetz. The rest of his music was on records. All through my growing up years, just about every Friday night, Dad would lie on the couch, or on the living room floor with a pillow, and listen to Isaac Stern, Itzhak Perlman, or Jascha Heifetz. I put on the Tchaikovsky.

My grandmother told me that my father could have been a professional musician. At Christmastime, when I was young, he used to take out his violin and play for the family. I remember one December when I was around Christopher's age, sitting on the couch and listening to him play "O Holy Night" while my grandma accompanied him on the piano. He knew the piece from memory. Dad's lips were stretched into a smile, his cheek pressed tightly against the violin as if he were hugging it. His eyes were shut. It looked like he was having the most wonderful dream, so I closed my eyes, too. I wanted to share it with him.

I used to love to listen to my father play. I'd watch his eyebrows go up when the music went high and furrow when it got fast. I'd stare at his rounded fingers as they moved up the fingerboard of his violin and wonder just how high a note he could make before he touched his chin. I'd follow his bow as it ran and bounced and danced on the strings. I was hypnotized by it. When I was a boy, sometimes I would sit quietly outside my dad's office at home with my legs pulled up to my chest and my cheek pressed against the door, listening to him practice. The sounds were smooth and warm and velvety. His violin, like a lullaby, soothed me. It sang warmth and security and connection — all that a child longs for. Once, as I listened, he opened the door, and I fell back onto the floor. As he stood over me, neither of us said anything. I noticed that his eyes were swollen; there were tears in them. I had never seen him cry before, but dared not ask why. As the years went by, I spent less time sitting outside my father's office. He took out his violin less and less, until eventually he stopped playing entirely — even at Christmas.

I adjusted the volume on the CD player. When I turned around, Dad was leaning back, his eyes closed. Tchaikovsky, like a familiar fragrance, had transported him to another place. He was somewhere playing his violin, I imagined. When Dad opened his eyes, he noticed me looking at him. Then he spoke.

"Michael . . ."

"Yeah?"

"Could you hand me my violin, please?"

I was shocked. "Now?"

"Yes, please."

"You want to play it?" I joked.

He twitched a smile.

Dad's violin case lay under his desk. I could see it from where I was standing. The leather was worn, and some of the stitching was coming undone. The brass latches were tarnished. I didn't know much about violins, but I'd heard that his was a good one. My father inherited the instrument from his mother's brother, Rudolph, who was once concertmaster for the Chicago Symphony.

I only met Uncle Rudy a few times when I was a child. He died young. I remember once when he visited, he taught me the parts of the violin: the scroll, the bridge, the neck, the ribs, and the belly, which made me giggle. Another time, he let me look through the *f* holes on the instrument to see the German maker's paper label and the small sound post, which he explained in Italian means "soul." And one Christmas, he took a candy cane off the tree and handed it to me. Then, holding my arms, he taught me how to conduct in 3/4 and 4/4 time with my new red and white baton.

I walked over to the desk and picked up the case with both hands. It felt strange to be holding it. I had only touched it a couple of times in my whole life. I laid it beside him and sat down on the chair. Dad ran his fingers across the case and thanked me. I was actually excited to see it; it had been a long time. Then he flipped up the latches and lifted the lid. He smiled when he saw it. I, too, was warmed by the sight of it.

The violin rested on a lining of crimson velvet. The varnish glowed like stained glass windows hit by the sun. As I looked at the instrument, my thoughts carried me to a Saturday morning at Joe's Tree Farm when I was about ten. Dad and I were walking through the rows when he began talking about the trees used for violin making. It wasn't like him to teach me things. I listened closely.

He told me that violin makers like to use young firs, pines, and spruces to make their instruments. Dad explained that many years ago craftsmen went into the forest and identified the trees that would make good violins by knocking on their trunks and listening to the vibrations carried within them. Sometimes, the violin makers had to wait many years for these trees to grow large enough to make them sing. As my father told me this, I could imagine him walking through the woods, knocking on tree trunks, and almost hugging them to listen. Yes, I thought, he would have been a good violin maker. Years later, when I recalled this lesson amidst the trees at Joe's, I smiled thinking that the very woods used for making violins also make the best Christmas trees, according to my father. No wonder he loved both.

Dad lifted his violin out of the case and set it gently on his lap. I could see that holding it gave him comfort. In the case was a small compartment. He opened the lid and pulled out a package of violin strings, rosin, and a key. Then he took out a folded white handkerchief. Dad always played with one under his chin. As he held the cloth, it appeared as though it was wrapped around something.

"What you got there?" I asked.

He looked up at me quickly, but didn't answer.

"What's that?" I asked again, pointing.

"Oh, nothing," he said. "Just an old handkerchief."

Dad put the things back into the case and shut the latches. Except the handkerchief. He set it on the nightstand behind the lamp. Then he turned and gave me a long look. "Michael . . ."

"Yes?"

He glanced down at the case then back at me, his lips pressed in a smile. "I'd like you to have this."

I stood up quickly. "Dad . . ." was all I managed to get out.

"Please."

I felt my chest contract. "Dad, no . . . I can't."

"If you don't take it," he said, grinning, "I'll have to use it as firewood."

I laughed, but I wanted to cry. Dad always used to say this. Whenever we begged him to take out his violin, he'd joke, "But we already have enough wood for the fire." I bit my lip. I knew what he was doing. He was starting to say his good-byes. I did not want to hear it. "Stop it, Dad!" I wanted to say.

"Michael, you're the musical one in the family."

I could feel the argument starting in my head. "I don't play the violin," I snapped.

"But Christopher does. You can give it to him someday."

He was right. Christopher had just started to play the violin. He was talented, too, like his grandfather. Christopher had a child's violin, but someday, if he continued, he would need another one.

"Please, Michael." His smile had melted.

With clenched hands, I shook my head. "Dad, no!" I almost yelled. I didn't want his old violin. I wanted *him*!

I saw his face crumble. I had wounded him.

Immediately, I turned away and walked toward the door. Blinking back tears, I steadied myself in the doorway. *I can't do this.* "I'm sorry, Dad." The words caught in my throat. "I gotta go. I'll see you later."

I sped down the stairs and into the living room. It was empty. I paced back and forth across the rug, sucking deeply at the air in the room. I sat down on the piano bench, pressed my head against the music stand on the piano, and began to cry. My torso shook with quiet tears. I cried for what I didn't have, for what I didn't know — for the years I spent wanting more. When the tears stopped, I sat there for a few minutes listening to my breathing. Finally, I raised my head.

The tree lights were on now, and so were most of the ornaments. Mom had hung more. Hooked on a branch in front of me was a piece of painted glass.

Every Christmas when I was young, I used to ask my grandmother to tell me the story. I knew it well. I reached out and touched it. Then I shut my eyes and remembered.

Chapter Six - The Shepherd

The church was warm. The air in the sanctuary was drenched with the scents of beeswax, pine branches set on the windowsills by the Altar Guild, and wet umbrellas. Boxwood wreaths wrapped with gold ribbon hung on the end of each pew. Garlands draped the white walls like icing on a wedding cake. Wool coats with heavy linings rubbed against each other as men, women, and children scrunched together in the pews. The men's knees butted up to racks with white offering envelopes and well-worn hymnals. Latecomers couldn't find a place to sit.

Tommy, dressed in a robe that his mother made from an old sheet, stood on the side of the sanctuary waiting to go on. Mathilda adjusted the cloth on his head and laid both hands on his shoulders.

"You really look like a shepherd," she said, smiling.

Then Tommy peeked from the side door and looked out into the church. Mary, Joseph, and the

Wise Men, all from the third-grade Sunday school class, stood around the manger, staring at a doll wrapped in a pillowcase. The other young shepherds had just arrived. It was almost Tommy's turn. The third Wise Man set his gift down beside the baby Jesus. That was Tommy's cue. The piano player started playing "While Shepherds Watched Their Flocks By Night." Mary, Joseph, and the Wise Men froze in a tableau, trying very hard not to move or giggle. Above them, an angel with an aluminum foil halo and cardboard wings looked over the scene. Soon, the lights dimmed. Mathilda squeezed Tommy's shoulders and kissed his cheek. "Play well, honey," she whispered.

Tommy entered the sanctuary. By the time he reached the platform, the church was dark except for the lights on the Christmas trees behind the altar and a footlight on the manger. A single spotlight came up on stage. The star of Bethlehem. Tommy walked into the pool of light and squinted because it was bright. He knew exactly what to do. He had practiced it all week in rehearsal.

All eyes were on the little shepherd boy as he lifted his violin up to his chin. He was only six years old. Mathilda crept into the back of the church and stood against the wall. Tommy looked up to the star and then, without accompaniment, began to play "What Child Is This?" As the sweet sounds of the shepherd's violin filled the room, the women in the pews took handkerchiefs out of their purses and dabbed their eyes.

All of a sudden, Tommy stopped playing. He forgot what came next. Everyone froze. Tommy tried again, but stopped in the same place. "Come on, Tommy," Mathilda said under her breath. All hearts were praying that the little shepherd would remember his piece. Tommy squeezed his eyes, thought very hard, and began again. But he just couldn't remember. Staring out into the church, he looked like he was about to cry. Anxiously, Tommy glanced over at the manger, then down at his violin. Now he had nothing to give the Christ child. His mother had told him that his music was his gift.

What will he do *now?* the audience wondered. Then suddenly, Tommy began walking over to Mary and Joseph. What's he doing? Mathilda thought. He was supposed to walk out into the spotlight, play his piece, then exit to the side of the sanctuary when he finished. He wasn't supposed to enter the stable. *What is he doing?* When Tommy reached the manger, he knelt down and set his violin and bow carefully on the straw next to the gold, frankincense, and myrrh. Then he left the stage.

Mathilda rushed to find him. After searching backstage and in the corridors, she finally discovered Tommy downstairs in the basement where he was hiding in the choir robe closet, crying. She held him as tears rolled down his cheeks. After a few minutes, Mathilda got Tommy's coat and hat, bundled him up, then drove home before the pageant was over. In the car, Tommy just looked out the window, his face pressed against the cold glass. When they arrived home, Mathilda took him into her bedroom, and they sat on the bed.

"I have something for you," she said, her arm tight around his shoulders.

Tommy looked up at her and sniffed. Then his mother reached above the headboard and took a small piece of light blue stained glass off the wall. It was a little larger than a postcard. The glass was thick, the edges heavily soldered. Painted on it was a shepherd holding a crook. He wore a blue vest, brown boots, and a red cap that fell over one ear. Three sheep rested at his feet.

"Here," she said. "This is for you."

As Mathilda placed the shepherd into her son's hands, Tommy's surprised eyes stared at the glass. It was the first time he ever held it. The shepherd had hung over his mother's bed for as long as he could remember. He thought it was beautiful. On nights when Tommy had a bad dream, or the sirens of the fire trucks woke him up, he would climb into his parents' bed. There he would ask about the shepherd, and she would tell him the story.

The year was 1922. When Mathilda was twenty-one and her only brother, Rudy, nineteen, they traveled from Chicago to Berlin to study music for one year — Rudy, the violin, and Mathilda, piano and voice. At that time in Germany, inflation was out of control. A suitcase of worthless German Marks wouldn't even buy a loaf of bread. People were hungry, but Rudy and Mathilda lived like a king and queen. They studied with the best artists in Berlin because they had American dollars.

Mathilda had a grand time in Berlin. Her days were filled with music lessons and practicing, letter writing, and dates with friends. Evenings were spent at concerts halls and theaters, restaurants and tea dances. For the entire year, she recorded the details of each day in a black diary that she kept locked. She purposefully wrote all her entries in English, not German. That way, if discovered, no one there could understand what she wrote.

One weekend before Christmas, Mathilda took a train to Cologne. She so wanted to see the city's famous cathedral. Both of her parents had talked about how magnificent it was. She had read that inside were the relics of the three Magi. When Mathilda approached the cathedral, she was absolutely awestruck. Never had she seen anything so huge. It was one of the tallest structures in the world, certainly the largest she had ever seen. Sections of the outer wall were still pockmarked with divots from bullets and shells — remnants from the First World War. Standing in its shadows, she gazed up, just as its builders had intended, and marveled at the sea of Gothic turrets and spires and pinnacles atop their flying buttresses. The two giant twin towers seemed miles away.

Mathilda entered the cathedral, where she stood quietly for a few moments in awe, taking in the vast open space, the soaring granite columns, and the sumptuous mosaics on the floor. Then she stepped over to a pew and sat down. The air was cool. At her feet, a wooden board was worn from centuries of kneeling. Along the wall, hundreds of dripping candles flickered on long metal racks. As she pulled the collar of her coat tighter around her neck, she watched a young man help a white-haired woman with shaky hands light a candle. In the distance, a group of women dressed a pink and black marble altar with silver candlesticks and a cloth of white lace.

Somewhere, a lone soprano rehearsed with a harp. Mathilda recognized the piece. The music quieted her spirit.

While she sat there, Mathilda's gaze swept the church. Large stone plaques engraved with dates and family names covered the walls. At the foot of the giant columns stood ornately carved wooden altars topped with marble angels, garlands, and statues of saints. Mathilda found herself thinking how everything was in need of a good dusting, then admonished herself for the thought and tried to think of something more holy.

Through the leaded stained glass windows, the setting sun bathed the cathedral in a symphony of colors. The windows reminded Mathilda of a kaleidoscope of jewels. On them were painted scenes from the Bible. She couldn't make out exactly which scenes all of them depicted, but it didn't matter. Such glorious windows, she believed, were not created to be studied as much as they were to be experienced.

After a while, Mathilda stood up and entered the south steeple. There, she climbed over five hundred spiraling steps to the observation deck, where the view was exquisite. Her father had told her not to miss it. Not only could she see the entire city, but Mathilda could observe the roof's intricate stonework, which was just as beautiful and finely crafted as that on the ground level. The craftsmen, she thought, must have built the cathedral as much for God's view as for man's.

Eventually, Mathilda descended the long staircase and walked outside to the main square. It was dark now. In front of the cathedral, crowds bustled in a large Christmas market, where strong-lunged vendors called out from behind piles of holly shaped into wreaths and crosses. Women with large baskets on their hips milled about in the cold night air, and pine-sellers carried greens slung over their shoulders and around their necks. Shoppers cozied up to stalls with carved wooden toys, handmade lace, candles, smoked meats, waffles, *glühwein,* and elaborate gingerbread hearts, houses, and generals riding horses with manes of shiny icing. The scents of cinnamon and cloves and ginger filled the air as snowflakes waltzed lazily in front of the gas lamps that had just been turned on. Overlooking it all, the cathedral's towers silhouetted the moon.

As Mathilda strolled through the stalls, she stopped at a table covered with pieces of colored glass. Each was painted with a different scene — angels, Nativities, bells, and Christmas trees. On one piece was a shepherd. Mathilda picked him up. His expression looked sad. Perhaps, she reasoned, he was the one left behind to watch the flock while the others went to Bethlehem.

"*Kann ich Ihnen helfen?*" (May I help you?) asked the man behind the table. His green wool coat and felt hat were covered with snowflakes. Some looked like the edelweiss embroidered on his hat.

"This is lovely," Mathilda answered in German. She spoke the language perfectly, but he could tell that she was not from Cologne. From Hannover perhaps.

"Did you paint it?" Mathilda asked.

"Yes."

"Did you paint them all?"

"Not all of them, but many. It's from the cathedral." The man looked up behind him. "From the chapel, I think, but we're not exactly sure. It's difficult to tell."

"But I thought you said that *you* painted it," Mathilda said, confused.

"I did," he answered. "All the pieces here come from the windows of the cathedral." He turned toward it. "As you can see, many of them were damaged during the war." He turned back and started brushing snow off the paintings. "We took the broken glass, cut it into small pieces, and painted pictures on them to help raise money to repair the organ."

Mathilda's eyebrows shot up. "The organ was damaged?"

"Yes. Badly."

She covered her mouth. It pained her to hear that. "I'll take it!" she said, handing him the shepherd. Mathilda reached into her handbag and started to pull out some German Marks. She paused, put them back, then took out three one-dollar bills. "Here," she said, handing him the money.

The man looked shocked. *She's American!*

"Oh, no," he said, shaking his head. "That's too much."

"Please. Take it."

"No, it's too much," he repeated.

"*Please* . . . for the organ."

After a pause, the man agreed. Dollars would be a great help. He thanked Mathilda several times as he wrapped up the shepherd in brown paper and twine. When he handed it to her, he removed his hat and gave a gentle bow. "God bless you, madam," he said. "And Merry Christmas."

When Mathilda returned to Chicago at the end of her year abroad, she hung the shepherd over her bed. There, he'd watched over her ever since. Oftentimes, when she told her son the story, she would look up at the piece of glass with a smile and say, "I have one of God's windows."

Tommy held his new gift as if a butterfly had just landed on his hand. "Thank you, Mommy," he said, softly. "Thank you so much."

Mathilda pulled him close and stroked his hair. Then she and Tommy walked into his bedroom. He set the shepherd against the lamp on the nightstand, and Mathilda tucked him in bed. After kissing him goodnight, she whispered, "God bless you, my little shepherd. You played beautifully tonight."

Chapter Seven

I adjusted a tree light so that it shone behind the shepherd. The light revealed tiny air bubbles trapped inside the rippled glass. Then I went back to decorating. Karen and Christopher would be there soon. I put wreaths on the front door and over the mirror in the entryway. I wrapped garland around the banister and set the paper choir that Carol made in school from folded magazines and Styrofoam balls on top of the piano. I hung our stockings on the mantel — first Dad's, then Mom's, mine, and Carol's. Her stocking came from the hospital. Since she was born close to Christmas, one day, when it was time to feed her, a nurse brought her to my mom in an enormous red stocking with white fur trim.

Next, I laid the red felt tree skirt around the tree stand and set up the crèche. We'd had the set for as long as I could remember. The stable was made of wood and the painted figurines of plaster. Joseph's head had been glued back on, and a couple of the sheep were missing. The roof of the stable was speckled white ever since the Christmas my mom let me spray canned snow on the living room windows and there was some left over. It looked like it had snowed in Bethlehem.

I smiled as I set out the figurines. As a kid, I used to play with them. Mom didn't like this very much because I'd add things to the nativity. One year, the Wise Men brought Jesus some Lincoln Logs. I also used to hide pieces around the house. (All the animals could fit inside my mom's purse.) And I'd make up adventures with the figurines, too. Once, the three Magi kidnapped baby Jesus. The donkey told Mary and Joseph where they were hiding, and the sheep scolded the donkey for telling.

When Carol and I were young, Mom would gather us in the living room on Christmas Eve, open her Bible, and read The Christmas Story. Before she started, she'd hand us the figurines. As she read, the two of us got to place them in the crèche. Carol always got Mary. I always got Joseph. We fought over the camel.

As I continued opening boxes and bins, I picked up a white shoebox off the floor. It wasn't labeled. I figured it contained decorations like the others. But when I opened it, I found some baby clothes and a few toys. I'd brought the box down by mistake. As I looked at the contents, I realized that they must have been my father's from when he was a child. I'd heard about some of these things, but had never actually seen them.

Sitting on the couch, I pulled out the tiny T-shirt and read the note my grandmother had pinned on it. (I recognized her handwriting immediately. The same writing was all over the pages of the piano books I used as a kid when she gave me my weekly lesson. Most of the time, she wrote, "Practice!") As I looked at the T-shirt, it was hard to imagine my dad being so small. Then I held up a lock of hair. It was definitely Dad's. His hair was curly as a baby, too.

I set down the ringlet and picked up a small stuffed lamb. Its nose and mouth were stitched with red embroidery thread. Tied around its neck was a droopy, faded yellow ribbon with a small brass bell. There was also a yellowed tag that said "Season's Greetings." I turned the tag over and discovered a handwritten note on the back. It said: *To my little lamb. Love, Daddy.* A heart and arrow were drawn beside the words. My eyes narrowed as I pondered the writing. This looks like *Dad's* handwriting, I thought. *But if it's my father's handwriting, it couldn't have been his lamb.* I stared hard at the toy and chewed on the inside of my lip, trying to make sense of it. *Who was my father writing to? And who was his little lamb?* Like too soft a whisper, I couldn't make it out.

Suddenly, there was a knock at the front door. I set the lamb down and peeked out the window. It was Carol. I got up and opened the door.

"Well, look who's here," I said with a big smile.

Carol stepped into the house with a vase of red roses and holly. The collar of her fitted black trench coat was turned up to reveal a Burberry plaid lining. She carried a chunky silver bag, and her big loopy silver earrings almost touched her shoulders.

"Merry Christmas," I said, leaning in to give her a squeeze and pretending to get caught in one of her earrings. "Well, I see you're wearing your old hula hoops."

Carol socked me on the arm. "Merry Christmas!" Then she kissed me on the cheek and wiped her purple lipstick off my face with her thumb. Her nails had rhinestones on them.

"What happened to your *hair*?" I cried, staring at her head.

She turned to the mirror, gave it a swish, and smiled brightly. "You like it?"

I screwed up my face. "Well . . . it's *red*."

She laughed heartily, running her hand through it. "For Christmas!"

Mom came in from the kitchen, wiping her hands on her apron, and froze when she saw Carol's new 'do.

Carol put her hand up. "Don't worry, Mom. It won't be this color for the wedding."

"Hallelujah!" Mom said, clutching her heart.

Carol handed my mom the flowers. "Merry Christmas," she said. Then she smirked. "Now, don't give it away."

Mom shook her head as Carol and I chuckled. Once, my dad gave my mother yellow roses for their anniversary. She took the flowers out of the vase and handed them all out at the old folks' home across the street from church.

"Come in. Come in," Mom said, walking into the kitchen.

Carol took off her coat and hung it on the banister. Then she stepped into the living room. Her high-heeled boots clicked on the hardwood floor. "Nice tree," she announced. My sister always said a good Christmas tree has the same qualities she looks for in a man: tall, no bald spots, smells good. And straight. She turned to me. "How's Dad?"

"Good," I answered. "He's sleeping. Is Jeff coming?"

"No. He's at his folks'."

Jeff was Carol's fiancé. The two had been engaged for almost a year. They met on an airplane. The way

Jeff explained it, he asked if he could have her dessert. She asked him to marry her.

We joined Mom in the kitchen, where the windows were all steamy. She had just put the boiled potatoes, milk, and butter into her Sunbeam Mixmaster.

"Ahhh. Smells great in here," Carol said, setting her purse down on the counter.

Mom opened the fridge. "Would you like something to drink?"

"That sounds good," Carol answered.

"What would you like?" Mom asked. Her back was turned.

Carol shot me a look and mouthed, "A *mar-ti-ni*." I stifled a laugh. Then she answered. "Tea would be nice."

From the beginning of Carol's engagement, Mom opposed the marriage. She said Jeff wasn't a "believer" and that a man and woman shouldn't be "unequally yoked." In fact, Mom didn't want to pay for the wedding, but Dad said that was nonsense. Carol was glad that Jeff wasn't coming over. It would be easier without him there.

To say there was tension in Mom and Carol's relationship was an understatement. Most of my life, it seemed that the two were at odds about something. According to my mother, Carol's tops were too low-cut, her heels too high, her music too loud, her circle of friends too wild. When Carol started smoking, my mom reminded her that the body is the temple of the Holy Spirit. The tattoo on her ankle did not go over well either. I couldn't remember Mom ever liking any of my sister's boyfriends. Carol likened their relationship to ever-shifting tectonic plates. Complete with fault lines.

Things got worse when Mom discovered that Carol and Jeff were living together. Carol did her best to keep it from my mother. When my mom found out, she stepped up her crusade. She called Carol on the phone every night to try and talk sense into her. She sent Bible verses and asked her Sunday school class to pray for her wayward daughter. As common as it had become, shacking up before marriage would never be acceptable to my mother. Carol didn't appreciate any of it and told my mom so. The only thing Mom seemed to like about the wedding was that they wouldn't be "living in sin" anymore.

Since my father's diagnosis, Carol and my mother's relationship began to thaw. Mom eased up. I figured Dad asked her to stop. He liked Jeff. I'm sure my mom also wanted to keep the peace. She didn't want to upset my father. Besides, Carol and Mom needed each other now. They depended on one another for support. Dad's illness had brought them closer. It bound us all.

After Mom poured Carol some tea, she turned on the mixer.

"You want me to do that?" Carol asked.

"No. No. You just relax."

Carol did not want to sit and make small talk. "Put me to work," she said, looking around the kitchen.

Mom thought for a second. "Well, if you don't mind, you can start setting the table. Oh, and could you bring me the serving dishes?"

"Sure." She was glad to have a job.

As Carol stepped into the dining room, I walked over to the mixing bowl and stuck my finger in the mashed potatoes. "And you get out of here!" Mom said, pushing me away. Laughing, I left the kitchen.

In the living room, I tidied up while Carol opened the buffet and pulled out napkins, candles, napkin rings, and silverware from a special velvet-lined drawer separated for forks, knives, and spoons. Then she opened the china cabinet.

My sister always loved the china cabinet. We inherited it from Grandma Mathilda. The oak piece, darkened with age, stood on ball and claw feet atop brass casters. Its bowed glass front played with the light in such a way that when you stood in front of it, your reflection looked like it was trapped inside the cabinet. In the door handle lay a tarnished key that Mom always kept in the lock. When you opened it, the cabinet smelled of lemon oil and Pledge. The shelves, with their narrow grooves in the back for plates and platters, were full of pieces one would expect to see in a grandmother's china cabinet: Hummel figurines, pink and blue Depression glass, bone china teacups with translucent rims you could see through when held up to the light, and silver serving pieces wrapped in plastic so that they wouldn't tarnish. Resting on doilies of tatted lace stood long-stemmed crystal goblets and porcelain dishes with the words *Rosenthal*, *Limoges*, and *Bavaria* stamped underneath. In the center of the cabinet, framed between two Lalique candlesticks, sat a crystal bowl on a spiraling base from the Steuben Glass Company.

Carol reached into the cabinet, pulled out the bowl, and carried it into the kitchen. Every Christmas and Thanksgiving, the bowl held Mom's cranberry and orange relish. When Carol was little, she used to ask Grandma about the pieces in the cabinet, and she would tell their stories in lavish detail. Some pieces she inherited. Others she picked up on her travels. A couple came from admirers. But Grandma never volunteered anything about the Steuben bowl.

Carol collected the rest of the dishes then stepped back into the dining room. A few ornaments still lay on the table. Mom hadn't finished putting them on the tree yet. Carol moved them aside then took two large pads for protecting the tabletop out from behind the dining room door and a gold and white damask tablecloth from the buffet. She placed the pads on the table then covered them with the cloth. On it were a few shadowy spots from past holiday meals that my mother could never seem to completely get out. She didn't mind. Mom called them "the ghosts of good times past."

After checking that the tablecloth hung evenly, Carol walked past the tree looking for the box marked dining room. When she found it, she took out a small plastic bag with some straw. She scattered the straw on the pads, covered them with the cloth, and began to set the table.

I always thought that everyone put straw under their tablecloths at Christmastime until one day in December my third-grade teacher, Mrs. Smith, asked us all to share our family traditions. I told her that we hid straw under our tablecloth because Jesus was born in a stable and there was straw there. Mrs. Smith looked surprised. Then she asked the class if anyone else did the same, and no one answered. I figured that they must not know much about Jesus because if they did, they would have put straw under their tablecloths, too.

When Carol entered the kitchen, Mom was setting a plate of food for Dad on a tray. On it sat a blue bud vase with some mums she'd cut from the back yard. Carol offered to take him his dinner and carried it upstairs. When she reached his office door, she moved the tray to one hand, knocked lightly, and stepped inside. Dad was awake.

"Hi, Dad," she almost sang.

His eyes lit up when he saw her. "Hey, how's my girl?" His voice was quiet.

"Good."

She walked over to his bed, set the tray on the nightstand, then turned and gave him a glossy smile. He looked thinner than the last time she saw him.

"How's Jeff?" he asked.

"Great," she said, enthusiastically. "He and Mom are downstairs right now dancing it up."

Dad laughed softly. He knew that Jeff was a sore subject.

"I brought you dinner," Carol said. "Turkey. And sweet potatoes." Dad could eat soft foods now. We were all glad about that.

Carol helped Dad sit up, spread the napkin on his chest, and handed him the plate and a fork.

"Thanks," he said. "It looks delicious."

"You're welcome."

While he ate, Carol took a seat and chatted about work and Jeff and how little success she was having finding a wedding dress. After a few bites, Dad set the fork down and leaned back. She could tell he was finished. She wished he had eaten more.

"All done?" Carol asked, standing up.

"Yes. Thanks." His smile broadened. "I'm saving room for pie."

"Good," she said, cheerily. She wiped his cheek with a napkin then set his plate on the tray. "Can I get you anything else?"

He looked across the room. "Well, actually . . . yes." Dad pointed to the wooden box on his desk. "There's a piece of paper in that box over there. It's rolled up. Could you bring it here, please?"

Surprised, Carol turned and looked. She'd never opened the box before. Carved on its sides were fleurs-de-lis, on the lid a knight's helmet and a crest. Carol walked over and lifted the lid. Inside were pencils, pens, a letter opener, a roll of stamps, and some loose change. She pulled out a scroll tied with string.

"This?" she asked, holding it up.

"Yes."

Carol brought it over to the bed and handed it to him.

"No," he said, putting one hand up. "It's for you."

Her eyes squinched. "For *me?*"

"I . . ." He cleared his throat. "I wrote it for you."

Carol stiffened. For a second she didn't know what to say. " *When?*"

"You'll see. Open it."

Carol looked down at the scroll then back at her father. Her smile was gone now. She was afraid to open it. Ever since Dad was diagnosed, my sister had done her best to hold herself together. And she thought she'd been doing very well. She hadn't cried when Mom called and told her it was cancer. She didn't fall apart when the doctor walked into the waiting room after his surgery and said, "There's just more there than we can deal with. We had to close him up." But this scroll, she feared, might be too much.

"Open it," he repeated. "I was going to give it to you on your wedding day, but . . ." He hesitated then handed her a smile. "I want you to have it now."

Carol and Jeff had suggested moving the wedding to an earlier date so that Dad could be there, but he said absolutely not. He did not want them to change the date just for him.

Carol sighed deeply, hoping to undo the tightness in her stomach. It didn't work. Then she sat on the foot of the bed. Full of emotion, she slid the string off the scroll, unwound the paper, and started reading.

Chapter Eight - The Scroll

The radiators in Tom and Shirley's Chicago walk-up crackled and popped as Shirley lay sprawled on the sofa bed with one pillow behind her back, a second propped under her feet, another between her legs, and a fourth under her head. The one pair of shoes she could still squeeze into was kicked off onto the floor. Slowly, she let out a long breath while holding her belly that she referred to as the bowling ball. The contraction had just ended. It was 4:00 a.m.

"How long since the last one?" she called out.

Tom looked at his watch. "Just about ten minutes."

"I think we should go now," she said, her face in a cringe.

"*Really?*" Tom said, jumping up from his chair. Shirley nodded, trying unsuccessfully to sit up. Tom rushed over to the sofa and grabbed her hands. He counted off. "Oooooone, twwwwwo, *three!*" Up Shirley went, and Tom held on for a second until she was steady.

"Thanks."

While Tom called a taxi, Shirley waddled over to the kitchen table and leaned against a chair. On the table sat her portable Singer sewing machine. It was duck egg blue. Spread out around it were several sheer pieces of a Butterick pattern pinned to blue and white checkered fabric. She was making a maternity skirt and smock, double-breasted with patch pockets.

"Ha!" Shirley shouted, staring at the white envelope that the sewing pattern came in.

"What?" Tom asked, as he started dialing their neighbor lady, Mrs. Ladney, to come over and watch Michael. Mrs. Ladney had been put on alert.

"The women on this maternity pattern have *thin* ankles!" Shirley glanced down in the direction of her own feet. She could barely see them. Her legs and feet had been swollen for months. She was sure there were patches on her legs that she'd missed shaving, and she had long given up painting her toenails. The week before, though, she wrangled Tom into painting them for her. As he did, Tom sang Christmas carols to the baby.

Soon, Mrs. Ladney arrived with her knitting. She was making booties for the baby. Shirley checked on Michael, and Tom grabbed Shirley's blue overnight case that sat ready by the door. In it was a cotton nightie, slippers, baby clothes, toiletries, and a pink quilted bathrobe with an embroidered collar. Earlier, Tom asked Shirley if she wanted to take along a couple of books to read while she waited. Shirley said, "Suuuuure!" and added that she could take her sewing, too. "Maybe I can finish it between contractions."

When they were ready to leave, Tom put on his hat and coat then helped Shirley with hers. It wouldn't go around her front. They said good-bye to Mrs. Ladney, who told them not to worry about a thing, then began their descent down the stairs. Shirley had to stop a couple of times to catch her breath. On the second floor, she felt another contraction coming on. Eyes clenched, she leaned against the railing and held on tight to Tom's arm. Tom didn't realize that he was clenching his face, too. Suddenly, Shirley started to laugh.

"What's so funny?" Tom said.

"Your face. It looks like *you're* the one having the contraction."

Tom laughed along with her.

When the contraction ended, Shirley asked, "How many minutes?"

"Eight," he answered.

She turned to Tom with a surprised expression. "*Eight?*" She tried to smile. "Do you know how to deliver a baby?"

When they reached the street, the two were slammed by the cold. The sidewalks were slick as glass. Across the road, Tom's De Soto hid under a blanket of snow. Carefully, Tom walked Shirley to the waiting taxi. The motor was running. He opened the cab door, tossed in the bag, and helped Shirley inside. The heater was on high. A picture of St. Joseph was clipped to the shade above the steering wheel.

"Passavant Hospital," Tom said, leaning forward. "My wife's in labor."

The cabbie looked in the rear-view mirror and announced, "A Christmas baby! How nice." And he drove off.

Shirley rested her head on Tom's shoulder as he held her hand.

"Your first one?" the cab driver asked, cheerily.

Shirley didn't open her eyes.

"Nope," Tom answered. "Second."

"I have two of my own." He flipped down the shade to reveal a photo of two boys waving Lone Ranger hats. Each had a crew cut; both were missing their front teeth. "Twins." Then he let out a jolly laugh. "But we didn't know it till my wife delivered." Tom looked worried.

Just then Shirley squeezed Tom's hand, lowered her head, and began taking deep breaths. Tom looked at his watch. Still eight minutes apart. The cabbie kept on talking.

"This is the first time I ever drove anyone to the hospital to have a baby," he said. "A lady almost gave birth in the back of my buddy's taxi. They were stuck in traffic, and she was screamin', and the husband was screamin', and my buddy was screamin'. He was afraid they were going to have that baby right there in his *cab*." The driver shook his head. "Whew-ee! Imagine that."

About a half hour later, and after another contraction, they arrived at the hospital. As the car pulled into the driveway, Shirley started breathing more normally again. So did Tom. He was very glad to be there. The driver pulled up to the curb, jumped out, and held the door while Tom helped Shirley out of the car. Snow floated down in thumb-sized feathers. After Tom paid, the cabbie patted him on the back. "Congratulations. And don't worry, sonny. Everything will be *just* fine."

Tom and Shirley walked slowly into the emergency room and up to the main desk. After checking in, a nurse dressed in a long-sleeved white uniform and white stockings with seams up the back helped the mother-to-be into a wheelchair and rolled her into an examining room, where Tom joined her. Shirley changed into a light blue hospital gown, and eventually a doctor came by to have a look. He said the baby would arrive in a couple of hours. The hospital called Shirley's doctor and moved Shirley into the labor room, where another woman waited with her husband. Shirley and Tom could hear them behind the drape that circled her bed like a shower curtain. As Shirley's contractions grew more and more intense, Tom stood beside her, holding her hand, stroking her head, and adjusting her pillows.

Finally, it was time for Shirley to be moved to delivery. As they pushed her bed out of the room, Tom kissed her forehead then grinned that grin of his. "Want your sewing now?" Shirley gave him a faint smile, put her hands on her belly, and half cried, "Don't make me laugh." When she was gone, Tom walked downstairs to the cafeteria to grab a sandwich and a cup of coffee.

After eating, Tom went to the Fathers Waiting Room, where two men with loosened ties were sitting on white vinyl chairs. One was snoring, and the other smoked. A large TV set in the corner was showing an old Bette Davis picture. Tom took a seat on the sofa.

On the coffee table lay newspapers, yellow-bordered *National Geographics,* and other magazines that the Friends of the Hospital donated after cutting the addresses off the bottom right corner of the covers. Tom held up a copy of *Good Housekeeping* and smirked at the man who was awake. "You think they're trying to tell us something?" The man chuckled while stubbing out his cigarette.

As Tom set the magazine down, a large black book sitting on the table caught his eye. It looked like an accountant's ledger. On the cover it said *The Fathers' Book.* Curious, Tom picked it up and started flipping through the pages. The book was full of journal entries written by men waiting for their new children to arrive. One soon-to-be father had written a prayer. Another wished for a son. A few wrote advice: "Learn to change a diaper" and "Don't wear a suit when burping your baby." A couple mentioned being constantly exhausted; one man called it the "baby hangover." And one father waiting for his third child wrote, "The day will come when you are leaving for work and your child blurts out, 'I love you, Daddy!' You won't want to leave."

At that moment Tom got an idea. He set the book down, stepped out, and asked for a piece of paper and a pen at the nurse's station. Then he walked back into the waiting room and began writing.

My Dear Baby,

I am sitting here at the hospital waiting for your arrival. It is snowing outside. I love you so much already and have not even seen you. Last night, I was singing, and your mommy said that you kicked. Maybe you were telling me to stop. I pray that you are healthy. I pray that you will grow up to be as kind and as thoughtful and as wonderful as your mother. I pray that you will not have my ears. I can't wait to see you.

Love,
Daddy

After reading over his note, Tom slipped it into his shirt pocket, then crossed his legs, leaned back, and waited.

Some people thought Shirley was going to have a boy because she carried the child so low. Others were sure it was a girl. Of course, Shirley and Tom would have been happy with either, but, secretly, Tom hoped for a girl. He already had his boy. A couple of hours later, a nurse stepped into the waiting room and called for Tom. She was wearing a tender smile. Tom's wish had come true. At 8:35 in the morning, Shirley gave birth to a healthy girl weighing seven pounds, six ounces. She came out screaming.

"When can I see her?" Tom asked, beaming.

"Right now," the nurse answered. "She's in the nursery. They're cleaning her up. When they're finished, they'll call you in."

"Thank you." On his way out, one of the men nodded his congratulations. The other was still asleep.

At the nursery, Tom stood in front of a large glass window. Behind it was a row of six bassinets. In three of them lay newborns wrapped tightly in blue- and pink- striped cotton blankets. Clear pockets on the tiny beds held cards with the babies' last names. Tom didn't see his.

In the back of the room, a nurse wearing a hospital mask stood at the counter with a newborn in her arms. In front of them lay a card with two tiny footprints stamped in black ink. That must be her! Tom thought. He wanted to tap on the window, but was afraid he might wake the babies. Just then, the nurse turned around, spotted Tom, and smiled under her mask. Tom pointed at the baby. "I. Think. She's. Mine," he mouthed. The nurse lowered her mask and mouthed back, "I'm almost finished."

Tom watched as the nurse dressed his child in a tiny white T-shirt, diaper, and cotton cap. Then she set his new daughter diagonally on a pink receiving blanket and began wrapping her. When the infant was all bundled up, the nurse held the baby toward the window and tilted her so that Tom could see. His face was one giant smile. The nurse pointed to Shirley's room, where she'd meet him. Tom quickly walked out.

Shirley was in a regular hospital room now. When Tom entered, Shirley attempted a smile. "Hi, Daddy," she said, softly. Tom walked over and gave her a gentle kiss on the forehead.

"Are you all right?" he whispered.

"Yes. Have you seen her?"

He was still beaming. "Yes. She's beautiful."

Soon the nurse came in with the baby and placed her on Shirley's chest. The new parents stared in silence at the miracle.

"What should we name her?" Shirley asked. They had boys' names picked out, but hadn't decided on a girl's.

Tom looked out the window at the snow. It was almost Christmas. "How 'bout Carol?"

Shirley liked it. Then she turned to their new child

and sang, "Hello there, Carol. Welcome to the family."

Later, Tom went home and called his mom with the good news. When he told her that she had a new granddaughter, Mathilda squealed, "Yay! I get to play dress up."

"Now, Mom," Tom bossed, "don't go buying a lot of things for her."

She gave a hoot. "Too late."

After talking with his mother, Tom rolled up the letter he had written to Carol and tied it with a piece of string he found in a drawer. He placed the scroll in the wooden box. Tom didn't know when he would give her the letter — someday when she was older, he thought.

After checking in with Mrs. Ladney, Tom got ready to return to the hospital. He showered and shaved and slapped aftershave on his face. He put on his best shirt and scratched his head, trying to decide which tie to wear. Normally, Shirley picked out his ties.

Just before leaving, Tom stopped at the kitchen cupboard and took out a bottle of champagne. A tag tied around the neck read, "For our new baby." As a wedding present, Tom's Navy buddies had given Tom and

Shirley a case of champagne. One day early in their marriage, Tom made some tags and tied them around each one of the bottles. The first tag said, "Anniversary of the day we met." The second read, "Anniversary of our wedding." The third was for Shirley's birthday and the fourth for Tom's. All the rest were marked, "For our new baby." He gave one to Shirley when Michael was born. Tonight's bottle was number six. Tom grinned as he closed the cupboard door. There were six more bottles to go.

At the hospital, Tom stopped at the gift shop and bought a narrow vase of white carnations and yellow daisies. When he entered Shirley's room, it was quiet. She had just dozed off. He didn't want to wake her. Her dinner tray sat on the nightstand waiting to be picked up. Beside the bed, Carol lay asleep in her bassinet. Tom set the flowers down then stepped over to his new daughter. Very carefully, he took Carol into his arms and kissed her forehead. She felt so warm. Tom marveled at her tiny hands, fingernails, and nose. Her delicate eyelashes — like petals. He tried hard to be happy, but in his heart he was torn between joy and sorrow. As he rocked his new baby girl, Tom closed his eyes and thought of another.

Chapter Nine

When Carol finished reading the scroll, she turned away and bit her lip. Then quietly, she began to cry. She couldn't hold her tears in anymore. Her daddy was dying. Her daddy would not walk her down the aisle. He would not dance with her at her wedding. He would never know her children. Her head rang with these thoughts.

Dad reached for Carol and pulled her to him. She lay her head on his chest and let herself cry. As her shoulders shook, he ran his hand over her hair just as he had done when she was a child after falling off her bicycle. When her tears stopped, Carol didn't get up right away. She remained still and felt him breathe. The beat of his heart and the clean smell of his pajamas comforted her. Finally, with a steadying sigh, she sat up and dabbed her eyes.

"Is my mascara running?"

He nodded.

"Dang them!" she said. "It's supposed to be waterproof."

They both laughed.

"I have to go downstairs now," she said, standing up and wrapping the scroll back up. "Dinner's almost ready." Then she leaned over and kissed him on the cheek. "Thank you, Daddy," she said, holding his arm. "It's beautiful."

He just smiled at her. His eyes were wet, too.

"You want some music on?" Carol asked, tucking in his blanket.

"No, thanks. I think I'll take a rest."

She could see that he was tired. Then she picked up the tray, stepped out of the room, and started to shut the door.

"Keep it open, please," he said. "It smells good."

Carol summoned a smile as she opened the door wider. Before going downstairs, she stopped in the bathroom to wipe her face.

In the living room, Carol searched the tree for a place to tie the scroll. She decided on a branch right next to the bride and groom. It made sense to put the scroll in the tree. It wasn't the first letter to sit on the branches. Resting in the needles lay several envelopes with six-cent stamps on their corners. They were love letters that my parents had written to each other their first year of marriage. Just weeks after they were married, Dad was deployed to the waters off Korea for three months. During this time, my parents wrote to each other every day. Each saved their letters. One year, Mom tucked several in the tree, and that became their home.

Early in our own marriage, Karen and I sat in the living room one Christmas and read the letters together. In them, Mom told Dad the latest scores from the sports page and explained the *Perry Mason* episodes he'd missed. She referred to herself as his "calendar wife," because in each letter she noted how many days, weeks, and months they'd been married. In one letter, she told my dad that he was going to be a father by explaining that "Aunt Martha" (what she called her time of the month) had missed her visit.

While Carol tied the scroll on a branch, I sat on the hearth trying unsuccessfully to light one of those fake logs, the kind where you light the wrapper and the log burns for hours. I turned around and noticed Carol staring at the tree. She was absorbed in her thoughts.

"You all right?" I asked.

My voice brought her back. "Uh . . . yes. Yes, I'm fine."

I spotted the lamb on the coffee table, leaned over, and picked it up. "Hey, was this yours by any chance?"

Carol shook her head. "No. It's cute."

"Look at this," I said, getting up. I held up the tag

so she could see. "Whose handwriting does this look like to you?"

Carol narrowed her eyes and read it. "Dad's."

"Exactly!" I looked down at the lamb's face. "But *who* would Dad have given a stuffed animal to?"

"Maybe it was yours."

I shook my head. "No. I'd remember."

Carol couldn't resist a grin. "Perhaps you were naughty one Christmas, and Santa decided not to give it to you."

I pointed at her. "Maybe they decided not to give it to *you*."

Suddenly, spotting an ornament on the lowest branch, Carol let out a scream. "You didn't!"

I tried to look innocent.

The ornament was a bear. One Christmas, Mom gave Carol and me ornaments from our alma maters. Carol's was a bear for Cal Berkeley and mine was a cardinal for Stanford. Cal and Stanford are huge football rivals. We decided that whoever's team won the big game got to hang their ornament higher than the other. We'd done so ever since. Well, Stanford had recently smeared Cal 21-3, so I hung my cardinal on the very highest branch and put Carol's bear way down on the bottom. It was sweet.

Carol knelt down to save her bear. "You think you

put it low enough?"

I let out a laugh. "Better get used to it."

At that moment, I noticed a car drive up in front of the house. "Karen's here," I announced.

Mom turned down the oven burners and walked into the living room. I grabbed a piece of mistletoe from the wreath in the entryway and opened the front door. Before stepping outside, I turned back to Carol. "Now don't go moving that bear while I'm gone." As I shut the door, I could hear Carol's laugh behind me.

When I got to the car, Karen was reapplying her lipstick in the rear-view mirror. Christopher was strapped into his car seat.

"Where've you been?" I asked, opening Karen's door.

She tossed me a fake smile. "Well, *someone* decided to go into the refrigerator and help himself to some milk and drink it out of the carton just like his daddy does. And then he proceeded to spill it all over his new Ralph Lauren sweater that Grandma got him for Christmas."

My nose wrinkled. "*Ohhhh.*" I looked over the seat. "Christopherrrr."

He giggled.

Karen put her lipstick away then stepped out of the car.

"Wow!" I said. "You look great." She was wearing

a new black dress and high heels, her reward for eating nothing but Jenny Craig for five weeks.

Karen looked down at herself. "You like it?"

"Love it."

She touched her top. "Too revealing?"

"Nope."

She pulled it up anyway.

Karen glanced at the house. "How's it going in there?"

"Fine."

"How's your dad doing?"

"Pretty well. Carol's here."

Karen gave a worried look. "How is she?"

"Good. I think she's on her third Valium." I opened the back door and leaned my head in. "Hi there, champ." Christopher was sucking on a candy cane. His hair was wet and freshly parted. I started unbuckling his seatbelt.

"We made cookies for Santa!" Christopher announced.

"You *did?*" I answered in a fatherly-shocked sort of way.

"And we put them on a plate with his glove."

I looked confused. "His *glove?*"

Karen piped in. "Yes, remember last Christmas Santa *accidentally* left one of his gloves in Christopher's stocking. Well, this year we're returning it."

"Ohhh," I said, giving a giant nod. "Now I remember. Good idea. I'm sure Santa needs that." I pulled Christopher out of the seat and set him on the sidewalk. Then I crouched down in front of him and held his hand. "Christopher, remember what I told you about Papa? He's upstairs sleeping, and we have to be *very* quiet. OK?"

"OK," he said.

I held up the piece of mistletoe. "And do you remember what I told you about mistletoe?" He stared at it. "This is it. Now, when you see Grandma, put it over her head and give her a *big* kiss. Like this." I held it above Christopher's head and kissed him loudly on his cheek. "Can you do that for Daddy?"

He nodded and giggled.

"Good." I handed it to him.

Karen grabbed a bag of presents off the seat, I pulled more out of the trunk, and the three of us walked up the driveway. The lights on the Christmas tree glowed behind the curtains. Somewhere down the street, carolers were singing "Deck the Halls."

As we approached the front door, I said, "I used to go caroling down this street by myself when I was a kid."

"By yourself?" Karen asked.

"Yes. I'd go in the afternoon when my mom

thought I was out playing and sing for the neighbor ladies." I grinned. "It was a great little business."

"What do you mean?"

"After each concert, I'd ask for a quarter."

We both stepped inside laughing.

"*Gueeeess* who's here," I announced.

Mom knelt down and stretched out her arms. Christopher ran over to her and held out his hand.

"Mistletoe!" she shouted. She gave Christopher a big hug then stood up with her hands on her hips looking surprised. "Now *where* did you get that?"

Christopher pointed at me. "Daddy!"

Mom acted shocked, and the rest of us laughed.

As Karen helped Christopher off with his coat, Mom sat down on the rocking chair and patted her legs. "Christopher, guess who called me tonight?"

He hurried over to his grandma and leaned on her knees, his face inches away from hers. "*Who*?"

"You'll never believe it," she said, slapping her heart. Then she widened her eyes. "Santa Claus." Christopher beamed. This was the third year in a row that Santa called Grandma on Christmas Eve. When Carol and I were children, he used to call, too. "He asked me if you were a good boy," Mom went on. Then she turned away and started nonchalantly plumping up a pillow to make him wait for her reply.

Christopher shook her knee. Smiling, she turned back to him. "I told him you were, of course."

Christopher's eyes were glued on her.

"Then," Mom continued, "he asked me what you'd like for Christmas. I told him that I would speak with you and call him back." She tilted forward. "So, sweetheart, what do you want for Christmas?"

We all knew. He'd been asking for weeks — more Legos, a bow and arrow, a toy microphone, and a frog. Santa Claus was ready. I'd been feeding the frog in my bathroom for a week.

Christopher looked toward the stairs and turned back. Then, tenderly, he said, "I want Papa to get better."

Mom gasped softly. Karen and I exchanged glances. My mother squeezed Christopher's hands and looked into his eyes. They were deep blue like his grandfather's. "I want that too, honey," she said. She squeezed a little tighter then looked up at me. "We all do."

Christopher adored my father. When he was a toddler, he'd crawl into his grandfather's lap while he was watching TV and just sit there. Sometimes, he'd sneak into my dad's office and ask him to play. Oftentimes, Dad was too busy, but once in a while he would put down his pencil and go to the family room, where they'd play blocks and laugh when the plastic Godzilla destroyed all the buildings. Christopher called his grandfather Papa. Dad called him Tiger. When I watched the two of them play together, I thought — *Who is this man? Where was he when I was that age? What changed him?* Was it the fact that he worked less now and had more time? Was it that second chance that comes with being a grandparent? Whatever the reason, I was grateful.

Christopher turned and looked at the tree. He stepped toward it and began to reach out for one of the ornaments. He stopped and turned to Karen.

"That's right, honey," she said. "Just look. Don't touch."

When I was his age, I, too, was dazzled by the Christmas tree's magic. Sometimes, I would lie under our tree and pretend that all the ornaments were alive. The Lilliputian instruments hanging on the branches played for the glass bulbs. The miniature ocean liner raced the locomotive. The cardboard animals wanted to eat the glass fruit. Somewhere my mom had a photo of me sleeping under the tree in my new pajamas. She snapped it after I fell asleep talking with the ornaments.

In my land of ornaments there was one leader, a toy soldier about three inches tall. Every year, the soldier hung on one of the highest branches of the Christmas tree, where he guarded all the other ornaments. A dashing little figure, he wore a plumed hat, high black boots, and a blue jacket with gold buttons and red epaulets. A sword hung from the sash wrapped around his waist. He played a drum, but with only one arm. Somewhere he had lost one — probably protecting another ornament, I reasoned.

As Christopher gazed at the tree, I spotted the little soldier up near the star and lifted him off the branch. Then I crouched down beside my son. The soldier rested in my palm. "This is the drummer boy," I said. "He's Daddy's favorite."

Chapter Ten – The Soldier

It was two days before Christmas 1944. Cyril and the other men from the 29th Infantry Division sat in a muddy trench in France waiting for orders. Twilight painted the sky red. Trees disappeared under the snow. The Germans waited on the other side. There were no blankets, no gloves. American supply trucks had been cut off. Cold was the second enemy. Cyril had worn the same filthy clothes for weeks. Every crease and thread of his uniform was caked with dirt, and his stubbled face hadn't seen a razor in days. His lips were peeled like old paint. Beside him, a gun sat at the ready.

To keep their spirits up, Cyril and a few other soldiers took turns describing what they wanted for Christmas dinner. One said honey-glazed ham. Another wished for fried chicken. A third, cornbread with bacon drippings, fried in Crisco.

Earlier that day, Cyril had written a letter to

Mathilda. He said nothing about the upcoming battle. He wasn't allowed to anyway. It wouldn't have gotten past the censors. Only in the closing did he write, "A big storm is brewing." He wondered if Mathilda would figure out what he meant. When Cyril finished writing, he slid the letter into his coat pocket. He didn't know when he'd get a chance to send it. Hopefully, he'd beat the letter home.

As the sun continued to set, a freezing wind sliced through the trenches. The talking stopped, and the men cupped their hands around their mouths and noses and breathed into them. Cyril pulled out a small black New Testament that Mathilda had given him the night before he sailed overseas. His name was embossed in gold letters on the cover. With shaking hands, he turned to the Gospel of Luke, chapter two, The Christmas Story, and started reading aloud. He tried to use different voices for the Angel of the Lord and the shepherds. He could see his breath as he read.

As the men listened in the fading light, their thoughts transported them to warm hearths, tender wives, and children unwrapping toy trucks and Erector Sets and Madame Alexander dolls by the Christmas tree. It was for all this, their captain had reminded them earlier, that they were fighting — for home and family and Christmas. When it got too

PHILLIP DONE

dark, Cyril stopped reading, closed his Bible, and put it back into his pocket. The red sky was now the color of lead.

Shivering, he wrapped himself tighter in his coat and repositioned his body in the frozen earth. As cold sank deeper into his bones, Cyril's thoughts drifted back to a sunny afternoon in Chicago. It was a few months after the bombing of Pearl Harbor, and America was heavily into the war. He and Tommy were walking home from the park. On each side of the street, old trees shaded houses with manicured yards and front porches covered with wicker furniture, rocking chairs, and porch swings. Tommy held a baseball in one hand and his mitt in the other. Cyril knew it wouldn't be long until he received his orders.

As they walked down the sidewalk, the two passed small red and white cloth banners with blue stars hanging in some of the windows. All over the country, mothers and grandmothers hung service banners like these in their front windows to honor loved ones away at war. Some of the banners were manufactured, but most were handmade. The stars were sewn on a background of white fabric, trimmed with a red border. Each star represented one person. Some banners had more than one star on them.

Tommy knew what the blue stars meant. His

parents had taught him. He had seen them in the drugstore window in town and at the barbershop where Cyril got his hair cut. Once, at the filling station, Tommy saw a man stand in front of a banner and salute it.

As they made their way home, Tommy stopped at a house. In the window by the front door, a service banner hung from a gold tasselled cord. The bottom edge was trimmed with gold fringe. In the center of the banner was a single blue star.

"Where is he?" Tommy asked.

Cyril looked at the house then turned to Tommy, confused. "What do you mean?"

"The star," Tommy said. "Where is he?"

It took Cyril a moment. "Ohhh," he said, understanding, "you mean the man who isn't home?" Cyril looked back at the house. "He's in Africa."

A little while later, Tommy spotted a second banner. On it were two blue stars. "Where are they?" he asked.

Cyril thought about it for a second. "One's in the Philippines . . . The other's in Europe. In Italy, I believe."

At the end of the block, Cyril and Tommy walked by a small brick house. A child's bicycle lay in the front yard. The lawn looked neglected. Tommy stopped suddenly. "Daddy, look!" he said, pointing to the window.

Hanging between the glass and drawn curtains hung another banner. But the star was not blue. It was gold. Tommy looked up at his father. "Why is that one a different color?" It was the first gold star he had seen. His parents hadn't told him about those. A gold star meant that a loved one had died.

Cyril stood silent, thinking of how to respond.

"Where is he?" Tommy asked.

Staring at the star, Cyril put his hand on his son's shoulder. "He's in heaven."

Cyril shifted in the trench, pulling his knees closer, when suddenly something in the mud caught his eye. He reached over and pulled it out of the earth. It was a small lead soldier. Cyril smiled at it. Where did you come from? he thought. Cyril held the soldier close to his face and examined it. His coat was blue. His tall black hat had a red plume. Around his neck hung a drum. The uniform looked French, Cyril thought. "Well, it looks like you're far away from home, too," he whispered.

Cyril checked to see if there were any other little soldiers in the dirt. There weren't. He was alone. "It's not good for a soldier to be without his regiment," Cyril said, softly. Then he pointed straight ahead. "The enemy's over there."

Rubbing the dirt off his new little friend, Cyril said, "How'd you like to go to Chicago? I know a nice boy there who'll take good care of you." He pretended to wait for a response. "Good." Then he tucked the soldier into his pocket behind the letter to Mathilda and patted his chest. "You'll be warmer in there."

When the war ended, the little soldier sailed across the Atlantic to his new home in America. It was his first voyage on a battleship. He stayed in a warm duffle bag for the entire trip. But the bag was not Cyril's. Cyril had not weathered the storm.

Weeks later, the soldier arrived in Mathilda's mailbox, along with the New Testament with Cyril's name on it and his last letter. One of Cyril's buddies had held on to them and waited till he returned home to send them to Mathilda. He explained in a note that these items were on Cyril's person when he fell.

After Mathilda received the package, she placed the contents in a manila envelope, along with Cyril's dog tags, medals, and the final telegram she received months before from the Department of War saying he had been killed. Then she set the envelope in the back of her dresser drawer and covered it with one of Cyril's sweaters. She never showed her son.

That same week, she took down the service banner hanging in her living room window, cut a star out of gold fabric, and stitched it over the blue one. The gold star was a bit smaller so it was bordered in blue. Then she hung it back in the window, where it remained for years after the war.

Only after Mathilda passed away and Tom was going through her things did he discover the envelope in her dresser. Alone in his mother's room, Tom read the note from Cyril's war buddy. He thumbed through the New Testament and smiled at the soldier in much the same way his father had on that freezing night when he first discovered it.

When Tom read Cyril's letter to Mathilda, his mind drifted back to an image of a brave boy watching his mother sitting in her rocker and wiping away tears while holding a telegram from the war department. He knew without asking what had happened. He wanted to run upstairs and hide in his room, but stayed and hugged his mother. He was the man of the house now.

For a couple of years, the toy soldier lived on a shelf in Tom's office. Then one December when he was tidying up, Tom took it down, blew off the dust, and walked downstairs, where he hung it on the highest branch of the

Christmas tree. He always sensed that it was intended for him. But what he didn't know — and would never learn — was that Cyril's last conversation about his beloved son was with this little leaden soldier who, from then on, would always watch over Christmas.

Chapter Eleven

As I hung the soldier back on the tree, Mom looked at Christopher and said, "How would you like to help Grandma in the kitchen? I need help putting sprinkles on a few more cookies."

"Yay!" Christopher shouted.

"Well, come on," Mom said. And she took him by the hand and left the room.

When they were gone, Karen set the packages she'd brought under the tree, I went back to my fire, and Carol started hanging icicles on the branches.

"You want me to help with that?" I asked Carol with a smirk. I knew how she'd reply.

She threw me a look. "*You* stay away from here."

I let out a laugh. In my family, there were those who placed each icicle on the tree one at a time (hangers) and those who tossed half the box in one fell swoop (throwers). Carol, Mom, and Dad were all hangers. I was the black sheep icicle thrower.

"Dang!" I shouted from the fireplace.

"What's wrong?" Karen asked.

"Only half this log will light. We have a lopsided fire."

"Ha!" Carol laughed.

At that moment, Mom walked into the living room holding up baby Jesus from the nativity. "Michael . . ." she said, stretching out my name. "Look what I just found." She tried to look upset. I acted innocent.

"Where was he?" Carol asked.

"In the refrigerator," Mom said. "With the eggs."

As everyone laughed, Carol walked over to the window, pulled back the curtain, and scanned the sky. After a few moments, she said, "Hey, Christopher. Come here quick." Christopher dashed into the room, and Carol pointed out the window. "There's the first star!" He jumped on the couch and looked outside. "See!"

In our house, when someone spotted the first star on Christmas Eve, it meant we could start eating dinner. When Carol and I were kids, we'd always stare out the window and search for the star. Whoever saw it first would point and shout, "I see it! I see it!" If the food wasn't ready yet, my mom would yell back from the kitchen, "It's just a plane. Keep looking."

"Well," Mom said, untying her apron. "It's right

on time. Dinner's ready."

Mom grabbed Christopher and helped him wash his hands. Carol lit the candles. I cut the turkey with an electric knife in the kitchen and filled the gravy boat. Karen hoisted Christopher onto his chair and tucked a napkin into his shirt. Soon, the turkey platter and bowls full of mashed potatoes and stuffing and cranberry relish and green beans and sweet potatoes with marshmallows on top surrounded plates, glasses, silverware, and freshly ironed napkins. I chuckled when I saw the sweet potatoes. When I was little, I got into trouble for pretending the marshmallows were snow and the little men I made from olives and toothpicks were skiing on it. Karen said she'd strangle me if I gave Christopher any ideas.

We all took our seats, Karen and I on one side, my sister opposite us. Christopher sat next to Auntie Carol. Mom sat at the end of the table across from Dad's chair. Seeing it empty was difficult for all of us. His place was fully set. Even though we knew he wouldn't be eating with us, when Carol set the table, she couldn't bring herself to leaving his spot bare.

As we unfolded napkins and placed them on our laps, Mom scanned the table, checking that she hadn't forgotten anything and that each bowl had a serving spoon. I picked up one of the rolls and turned it over.

"Good," I said. "They're burned."

"They are not!" Mom protested, fake offended.

It was a Christmas tradition that my mom burned the rolls. The timer on her oven seemed to take the holidays off. Most Christmases my father would shout, "Sug, is something burning?" then Mom would run to the oven and pull out a tray of black-bottomed rolls.

For a moment, no one spoke. Carol, Mom, and I were all thinking the same thing. This was the time when my father would have said grace. Typically, he didn't like to pray out loud and left that to my mom. But on Christmas, he prayed. Dad's prayer was always short and simple, like a child's. And it was always the same. First, he would thank the Lord for all our blessings. Then he'd give thanks for each of us individually. When he finished, he'd raise his head, announce, "Let's eat!" then reach for the mashed potatoes.

Carol and I looked at each other, then at Mom. She gave an understanding smile and laced her hands together. We bowed our heads.

Mom prayed for Dad and for each one of us. She prayed for strength. As she talked with God, I watched her face. She looked tired. The emergency runs to the hospital and the months of worry had taken their toll.

There was much she didn't share with us — the hours curled up on her bathroom floor begging God to save her husband, the shattered nights crying into his pajamas that she kept under her pillow. But nothing had been more difficult for her than the guilt. Grief and guilt, she told me one night on the phone, are married. Not a day went by that my mother didn't wonder what she could have done differently to help my father. She was a health care provider, trained to prevent disease from spreading. Mom prayed for comfort.

After she finished her prayer, Christopher said "Aaa-men!" and the room filled with laughter. Then arms reached, and we began passing around the dishes and said what we always did when gathered at the dining room table: Mom asked if the gravy was warm enough; Carol commented on how delicious everything was; Karen asked for the recipes, and I reminded Christopher to use his fork.

Together we talked and laughed so hard that we cried. We cracked up recalling the Christmas Eve when my mom decided we'd have carp for dinner, and I walked into the bathroom and just about had a heart attack because the tub was full of live fish. We burst out laughing when Carol reminded everyone how Mom used to spray the house with Windex before

Dad came home so he'd think she had cleaned the house. We laughed some more when Mom shared the family fruitcake story. When my uncle was in the Korean War, my aunt made him a fruitcake for Christmas. It arrived months late. My uncle shared it with his buddies. The fruitcake had fermented, and his buddies got drunk. They asked my aunt to send another one.

When dinner was over, Mom went into the kitchen to get dessert ready, and Karen and I started clearing away the dishes. Carol set out new plates while Christopher played in the living room. As whipped cream whirred in the mixer, Mom called out, "Who wants dessert?"

We all answered "Me!" at the same time.

Everyone loved my mom's pumpkin pie. Though she used the recipe on the Libby's can, hers was the best I ever tasted. She had a secret ingredient: nutmeg. Mom said it wasn't called for in the Libby's recipe, but Grandma Mathilda always put nutmeg in her pumpkin pie, so my mom did, too.

We all took our seats again as Mom carried in the pie and the whipped cream. When Karen called Christopher back to the table, I noticed that he was holding the lamb.

"Christopher," I said, reaching out my hand, "give

that to Daddy, please. It's old."

I turned to Mom. "Do you know anything about this lamb? I found it in a shoebox." I got up, grabbed the box, and brought it over to her.

She glanced at the lamb. "That was your father's when he was a child."

"I don't think so," I said. Then I showed her the backside of the tag. "Look at this."

Mom held the tag out in front of her and lifted her chin like she always did when she tried to read something without her glasses. As she looked at the tag, I searched her face. Her expression shifted from curious to puzzled. Mom read the tag again. Her forehead wrinkled as she considered it. When she set down the lamb, the confusion had left her eyes.

For a brief moment, I could see that she didn't know what to do next. She sensed we were all looking at her. Avoiding our eyes, she ran her fingers over her pearls. Then she picked up the serving knife, looked across the table, and forced an unconvincing smile. "Karen, some pie?"

Carol and I swapped quick glances.

"Yes, please," Karen answered.

Mom knew something. *She knows something about this lamb.*

"And Christopher," Mom continued. "Would he like some?"

"Yeah!" Christopher shouted.

"Just a little piece," Karen answered. "Thank you."

I stopped her. "Mom!" She turned and looked at me as though we were not already in the middle of a conversation. "Is there something you're not telling us?"

Her smile had fizzled away. Then she set down the knife and put her hands in her lap.

"Michael," she said, quietly, "I haven't seen that since before your dad and I were married. I always assumed that it was his play toy. I never read the tag before."

"Do you know whose it was?" I asked.

Silence.

Then, after letting out a long breath, she said, "I do now."

My eyebrows lifted. "You *do*?" Carol stopped in the middle of a sip and put down her glass. Karen excused Christopher from the table. We waited for an answer. "Mom, tell us."

"I don't know if I should," she continued. Her voice sounded nervous. "It's really not my place to say." She closed her eyelids tightly like a child who is praying really hard.

I placed my hand on hers. "Mom, it'll be OK."

There was a long pause. Then, looking down at her plate, she began to explain. "There was another child."

All eyes shot open.

"You and Dad had another baby?" Carol rushed to say.

Mom turned to her with a frosty look. "Not your father and I," she snapped. "Your father had a child before we were married."

My breath stopped. I flashed a look at Carol then swung it back to Mom. "Uh . . . *when?*" I stammered.

Mom pressed her fingers on her lips. "When he was in college."

"Oh, my *God!*" I said, shaking my head and slumping back in my chair.

Karen put her hand on my thigh.

"A boy or girl?" Carol asked.

"A girl."

Carol gasped, covering her mouth.

I threw up my hands and announced, "Merry Christmas, Michael. You have another sister!"

"Michael!" Karen protested.

"Sorry," I said, shaking my head. "Sorry."

We all sat in stunned silence until Carol broke it. Her voice was gentle. "Mom . . . what was her name?"

Mom turned to Carol and smiled feebly. "Kathleen . . . Kathleen Marie."

Chapter Twelve - The Lamb

After Tom finished his last class for the day at the University of Chicago, he took the elevated train, or "the L," downtown and went for a walk. He liked to go for long walks when he had a lot on his mind. As Tom lumbered down the street, heavy sheets of rain poured off his umbrella. Along the sidewalk, holiday shoppers crowded under striped awnings, waiting for a break in the weather.

It had been a difficult year. In March, Tom married his college girlfriend, Sarah, at the Cook County Courthouse after they found out she was expecting. He felt it was the right thing to do. The baby was delivered at the medical school by an intern; they couldn't afford a doctor. Tom was only twenty years old. Sarah was eighteen.

When Tom learned that Sarah was pregnant, he knew it would be difficult to tell his mother. What he hadn't anticipated was how heartbroken he would feel. He fought back tears as he told her the news. Mathilda asked Tom what his plans were, where they would live, and how they would support the baby. Tom said that he would marry Sarah right away and get a job; the rest he hadn't figured out yet.

Mathilda said that Sarah could move in with them, and Tom was grateful for the offer. He never would have been able to afford an apartment. The house, a two-story, three-bedroom Victorian that Mathilda and Cyril bought when they were first married, had plenty of room. There was a large living room, where Mathilda gave piano lessons, and a wrap-around porch, where in the summer, she liked to have her Happy Hour. "I'll sleep in the guest room," Mathilda said. Then she smiled. "Besides, I like the mattress in there better anyway."

Sarah's parents, on the other hand, were furious. They refused to attend the wedding ceremony and did not see the baby when she was born. The only time they had seen Kathleen was when Sarah surprised them with a visit. Even then they would not hold the child.

As Tom walked in the rain, he thought about his future. He'd finish school in a year then get a job. Hopefully, Sarah would go back to school. After the baby was born, she dropped out. Perhaps after Tom graduated, he would join the Navy. He had always wanted to be in the service like Cyril had. Things would get better, he thought. They had to.

Eventually, Tom found himself on State Street in front of Marshall Field's, the largest department store in Chicago, near one of the landmark cast-bronze clocks that guarded the corners of the thirteen-story building. The light from the store's windows reflected on the wet sidewalk. When Tom was a child, Mathilda used to take him there every December to look at the Christmas windows. One year, he watched mechanical elves build toys in Santa's workshop. Another year, life-like snow fell on gingerbread cottages while polar bears and penguins skated on mirrors of ice. It was always magical. Afterward, he and Mathilda would wait in line to see Santa Claus then ride the elevator up to the Walnut Room, where he would gaze upon the Giant Tree laced with thousands of white lights and dripping with ornaments. Sitting near the tree, Tommy would drink hot chocolate served by men in black bow ties and eat a pink marzipan pig while a pianist played on a shiny Bösendorfer grand.

As the rain dripped from his umbrella, Tom stopped in front of one of the windows. Behind it stood a Christmas tree packed with red and gold balls, iridescent nuts, and fruit fashioned out of glass. On a white velvet tree skirt sat the most lovely toys: a china tea set, a dollhouse with electric lights, a huge taffy-colored bear, a Raggedy Ann, and a puffing railway that dashed around a circular track. How wonderful they all looked, he thought. He wished that he could buy any one of them for Kathleen. She didn't have many toys. There had been no baby shower, no baby book filled with cards and lists of gifts. Her crib was empty except for a pink blanket that Mathilda knitted.

Taking in the scene, something near the top of the tree caught Tom's attention. He stepped in and put his hand over his brow to get a better look. It was a little lamb. Tom smiled at it. Then, he pulled out his wallet and counted his money. He had a little more than ten dollars. Mathilda had given it to him for next semester's books. He knew he probably shouldn't spend the money, but every child should have a stuffed animal, he thought. Besides, Tom hadn't gotten her anything for Christmas yet. He closed his umbrella, took off his hat, and stepped into the store's large double doors.

Inside Marshall Field's, customers bustled about and waited in long lines while tired clerks punched keys on loud registers and Bing Crosby sang over the loudspeakers. On shiny beveled glass counters stood mirrors and lamps and enormous black urns filled with white poinsettias, magnolia leaves, and holly. In the aisles, high stacks of tins and boxes with labels from Paris and Vienna and Istanbul sat on marble-topped tables. Elevators with uniformed girls transported shoppers from floor to floor, where garlands swung along the walls and silver reindeer flew under the Tiffany glass ceiling. Everywhere it smelled of pine and fancy soap and the scents of hundreds of perfume testers squirted on the wrists of gloved women.

Tom took the elevator upstairs to the toy department, named Toy Land, where a large sign announced how many days until Christmas and dazed parents pulled kids' hands away from paper dolls and yo-yos and Candy Land. In the center of the floor, beside posts decorated with giant candy canes and lollipops, clerks dressed as elves passed out sweets to little ones as they waited in line to have their photos taken on Santa's lap. After walking through aisles of games and puzzles and picture books, Tom found the stuffed animals. On the crowded shelves sat cats and dogs and bears and lions and giraffes and zebras in every imaginable size and color. He never realized there were so many. Near him, a young boy was promising to be good forever if his mom bought him a stuffed monkey.

Tom found his little lamb on the top shelf. It was made in Germany by the Steiff plush toy company. Tom knew it would cost a lot. Mathilda had told him that these hand-sewn animals were the best in the world. Actually, she had a small Steiff bear of her own. His name was Max. Mathilda took him with her whenever she traveled abroad. Once at a bridge party, Mathilda shared with her lady friends that she would be traveling on her upcoming trip to Europe with her companion, Max. She purposefully didn't elaborate. A couple of eyebrows shot up around the table. Mathilda just grinned and continued playing cards.

Tom picked up the lamb and read the price tag. It *was* expensive. For a few moments, he pondered whether or not he should buy it. Maybe he could find another just like it for less somewhere else, he thought. Reluctantly, he set the lamb back and walked away. But halfway down the escalator, he changed his mind. *Kathleen just has to have it*! He turned right back around, sprinted up the escalator backward, and grabbed his lamb.

When he got to the register, the clerk asked Tom if he wanted it wrapped special, but he was afraid that he wouldn't have enough money, so he said no. The customers behind him waited as Tom put his last few nickels and dimes on the counter. He had thirty-five cents to spare. On the way home, Tom held the dark green shopping bag with the emblem of the cast-bronze clock on his lap so that everyone on the Elevated could see that he bought his daughter a real Steiff lamb at Marshall Field's. Someday he would take her there to have her photo taken with Santa Claus and see the Giant Tree in the Walnut Room. And afterward they would drink hot chocolate and eat a marzipan pig.

When Tom arrived home, Mathilda was giving a piano lesson and Sarah was on the phone in the kitchen. Tom waved hello, then walked upstairs to his and Sarah's bedroom, where Kathleen was sleeping in her crib. The room was dark except for the light of a street lamp squeezing through the gap in the drapes. Tom sat on the bed and turned on the lamp. Downstairs, Mathilda's student was playing her scales.

Tom couldn't wait till Christmas to give Kathleen his gift. He was too excited. As he pulled the lamb out of the bag, he spotted some ribbons, bows, and tags with red string on the dresser. Sarah had been wrapping gifts. He jumped up, grabbed a tag, and sat back down on the bed. Then he took a pen out of his pocket and wrote a message on the back of it. Next to the words, he drew a heart and arrow and colored them in. After tying the tag around the lamb's neck,

Tom stepped over to the crib with his gift and looked down at his daughter. She was fast asleep.

"Hi, baby," he whispered, softly. His face looked so loving. "Daddy brought you a present." Smiling, Tom held it over the crib. "It's a lamb."

Kathleen didn't move.

"It goes *bahhh*." Then he put the toy close to his face and said, "*Bahhh*" again. "Its head turns, too." He swiveled it. "See?"

Then Tom crouched down beside the crib and peeked through the bars. His face was close to Kathleen's. He could hear her breathing. Her little lips quivered while she slept. For a few moments, Tom stayed there just watching his beautiful little girl. Finally, he stood up and laid the lamb at the foot of her crib. After he tucked Kathleen in, Tom walked quietly out of the room and closed the door.

Chapter Thirteen

Kathleen Marie. The name hung in the air as I stared at the red wax dripping down the side of a candlestick. At that moment, I felt exhausted. The news pressed down on me like a heavy lid. All of a sudden, Karen pulled something out of the box. "Look at this," she said. Her voice broke my thoughts.

Everyone turned and stared at the object in Karen's hand. She held up a baby bracelet. It was beaded, the kind all babies used to wear in hospitals to be identified. On some of the beads, letters spelled out my family's last name. It *had* to be Kathleen's. We knew that immediately. The beads were pink.

Karen passed the bracelet to me, and I handed it to Mom.

"I never knew that was in there," Mom said.

"Wait," I said, trying to make sense of it. "Wait. You say Dad had another child in college . . . Was he married?"

Mom nodded. "Yes . . . but the pregnancy came first."

Carol cocked an eyebrow.

"What was his first wife's name?" Karen asked

"Sarah," Mom answered.

"What happened to them?" Carol asked.

Mom took in a breath and exhaled while we waited. "After they found out Sarah was expecting, they got married and moved in with Grandma."

I looked surprised. "They lived with *Grandma*?"

"Yes. One day Sarah went to visit her parents with the child, and they never returned."

"Oh, my God," I whispered. I started to feel my pulse in my chest.

Karen shook her head. "How awful."

Carol cut in. "How long were they married?"

"Not long," Mom answered. "I believe they began divorce proceedings soon after that."

I spoke before I had a chance to breathe. "But . . . but what about the baby?"

Mom turned to me. "Her parents pressured your father to give up his rights to the child."

My eyes gripped hers. "But he didn't, did he?"

She nodded. "Yes."

Feet uncrossed under the table.

"But *why*?" I cried.

"They wanted nothing to do with your dad. Her father was well established in the community . . . a politician, I think. The family had money."

"But what about Grandma?" Carol demanded. "Didn't she try to stop it?"

"No," Mom replied. "She advised your dad to give up the child."

"I can't believe this," I said, digging my elbows into the table. "How could Dad *do* that?"

Mom's back straightened. "Michael, Sarah's family had a lot of power and influence. Your dad *had* to sign the papers."

I just shook my head.

"You have to understand," Mom went on. "Things were different back then, not like they are today. Your dad was a kid himself. The adults told him it was the best thing to do, and he listened to them."

Suddenly, an image flashed into Carol's mind. "The bowl!"

We all turned to her.

"What are you talking about?" I said.

Carol pointed to the Steuben bowl on the table. "Grandma's bowl!" She began to speak quickly. "I used to ask Grandma where it came from, but she'd never tell me. She was always evasive, like she was covering something up. But once when I asked, she said, 'That piece came from a woman who loved your father very much.' I'll never forget it." Carol stopped talking and looked hard at the bowl. "It's from Sarah. I *know* it is."

A flare of goose bumps prickled my arm. "Is that true?" I said, turning to Mom.

She shrugged. "I don't know. I don't know anything about it."

Carol slapped her hands on the table. "I'm sure of it!" She looked at Mom. "Normally, Grandma told me *everything* about her things. But not this bowl. She didn't want me to know. Sarah *must* have given it to her."

"But this bowl's expensive," Karen chimed in. "Sarah was a college student."

Carol turned to Karen. "Her father could have cut off her money when she got pregnant," she reasoned. "Maybe Sarah gave Grandma the bowl early on when she was first getting to know Dad. Mom said Sarah's family had money."

Everyone fastened their eyes on the bowl like guests at a séance gazing at a crystal ball. It was strange to think that for all these years something from my father's first wife sat in the center of our dining room table. Most families keep their skeletons in the closet. Ours was in the china cabinet.

Suddenly, realizing that she hadn't served the pie, Mom stood up and started passing it out.

"Did Sarah keep the baby?" Carol asked as she took her plate.

"I've said too much," Mom answered. "Your father should tell you these things."

I put my hand on her wrist. "Mom, please. You can't stop now."

Mom stopped cutting and her eyes roamed over my face. Then she turned back to Carol. "We're not sure. She may have stayed with Sarah. Your dad believes that her family forced her to give the child up. Sarah's parents pushed adoption from the beginning. It killed your father."

"Did he tell you this?" I asked.

"He didn't have to," Mom answered. "You know your Dad struggled with his own adoption. I've told you that. It was the *last* thing he ever wanted for his child."

I leaned back in my chair and ran my fingers through my hair. My mind was flipping from past to present. Clenched thoughts began to rearrange themselves, and suddenly certain things started to make sense. It all started to come together — his quietness, his refusal to speak about the past, his avoidance and isolation. No wonder he stopped playing his violin. His song had been silenced.

"Did Dad ever try to find her?" I asked.

"Oh, yes. For years. But he was never able to."

Carol poked a fork at her pie. "Did you ever speak to Grandma about it?"

"Only once. I remember she said, 'Some things are better as if they never happened at all.'"

Carol nodded. "That sounds like her."

I rubbed the back of my neck. "Did Dad talk about it much?"

"Not a lot. He kept it to himself mainly. When we were first married, sometimes he would look at a little girl and say, 'Kathleen would be that age now.' He sounded so sad." I heard a new gravity in my mother's voice. "I always felt bad because there was nothing I could do. It haunted him."

"Why didn't you and Dad tell us?" Carol asked.

Mom put her head down and wiped her eyes with a napkin. I could see that it hadn't just haunted my father.

"I'm sorry," she said, sniffling. "This isn't easy for me." Pressing her lips together, she breathed in and out slowly. "Your father didn't want you to know. He was ashamed, *terribly* ashamed. He was afraid that you'd think he was a bad father."

I turned and looked upstairs. That poor man. The

pain he must have carried from losing a child in that way, coerced into surrendering her, then feeling that he couldn't speak to anyone about it. My heart ached for him. I turned and watched Christopher playing with his cars on the kitchen floor. I couldn't imagine losing my son. It would destroy me. At that moment, I wanted to run upstairs and tell my dad that I knew and throw my arms around him and hold him and not let go. No wonder he closed himself off. No wonder he wasn't present so much of the time. He was deviled by a secret. He'd been robbed of his child.

Just then my eyes fell on my parent's wedding photo on the piano.

"Mom, does this have anything to do with your parents not going to your wedding — because Dad was divorced?"

She nodded. "Yes. When my parents found out, they didn't want me to marry him. The first year of our marriage, my mother didn't want anything to do with him." Managing a weak smile, she patted my hand. "But after you were born, she came around." Mom began cutting a small piece of pie. "I'm going to take a slice to your father."

"Are you going to be all right?" I asked.

"Yes. Thank you." She inhaled deeply, trying to bring back a smile. "It's better that you know."

After Mom left the table, Carol, Karen, and I sat there for a few moments in concentrated silence. Fiddling with my spoon, I looked up at Carol and shook my head in disbelief. "We have a sister." Carol just nodded. Karen stood up and started massaging my shoulders.

As I rubbed my eyes, a hurry of thoughts carouseled in my head: *What does Kathleen look like? Where does she live? What has her life been like? Does she have children? Maybe I have nieces and nephews.* I looked up at my sister. *Perhaps Kathleen looks like her.* Suddenly, I pushed my chair back and stood up. I had the urge to find out more.

"I'm going to talk to Dad."

Carol's eyes widened. "*Now?*"

"Yes."

She looked worried. I could tell that she didn't think I should confront him.

I worked to keep my voice soft. "Carol . . . we have a sister. Don't you want to know more about her?"

"Yes, but . . ."

I leaned over the back of the chair and looked straight into her eyes. "Carol, Dad is *dying*. If I don't ask him now, we may never find out."

After a long exhale, I picked up the lamb and the shoebox, walked through the living room, and up the stairs. I put the lamb into the box then pushed opened the office door. Mom was seated beside the bed. Seeing the shoebox, she knew what I was planning to do. I set it on the desk. Mom stood up and said she needed to start on the dishes.

When she was gone, I walked over to the windowsill and started playing with some of the ornaments. Mom had brought a few up and set them on the branches.

"How was dinner?" Dad asked.

"Great. Mom burned the rolls."

It made him smile.

As I stood there, tears pressed behind my eyelids. I didn't know how to begin.

"You know what I just remembered?" I said, trying to keep it together. I gave a little laugh. The tears pushed harder now. "I remember when you took the family to hear the *Messiah* for the first time. I think I was about six or seven. I thought you were crazy." I wiped an eye. "The orchestra started playing the introduction to the *Hallelujah Chorus*, and you stood *up*!" My laugh sounded like crying. "Remember? Right in the middle of the concert, in front of thousands of people, my dad stands *up*! I didn't know you're supposed to stand for the *Hallelujah Chorus*."

As Dad laughed softly, I spotted a familiar looking

ornament on the windowsill. It was a red construction paper heart. I remembered cutting it out in first grade. The class was making Mother's Day cards. I asked my teacher, Mrs. Gonzales, if we'd be making cards for Father's Day. She said no because Father's Day was in the summer. Later, when she walked by my desk, she stopped and smiled. On my card I had written "To Dad, Happy Mother's Day."

Holding the ornament, I started to have second thoughts. Perhaps it *was* too late. Maybe I shouldn't ask him now that he was so ill. I didn't want to upset him. Maybe it was a bad idea. I was afraid to bring up Kathleen. Surely, he wouldn't want to talk about her. My whole life he never opened up. Why would he now? This is going to be like every other conversation we never had, I thought. *What was I* thinking? I set the ornament down, took the box, and started toward the door. I couldn't do it.

"Michael . . ." I stopped. "Michael, wait. Come sit for a moment."

I just stood there, my hands gripping the doorframe.

"Please, Michael . . . sit with me." Head down, I walked over to the bed and sat beside him. He waited for a long moment before he continued. "Your mom told me what happened."

Immediately, it felt like all the air had been sucked out of the room. I could feel my heart tolling in my head. *Would he continue?* He turned away from me. Then, softly, he began to speak.

". . . I tried to find her, Michael."

Oh, my God. He's talking.

"I want you to know that I tried to find her." The end of the sentence caught in his throat.

I released a breath I didn't realize I'd been holding. *He's speaking about Kathleen!* "I know, Dad," I said, quickly. "I know you tried."

He was still looking away, his head tilted toward the window. I opened the box and pulled out the lamb. He turned and smiled at it. Then I found myself speaking.

"Dad, tell me what happened." He didn't respond. There was a long silence. One heart beat. Then another. I felt as if I were protecting a struggling flame with my hands, trying not to let it go out. "Please, Dad." I could feel my Adam's apple rise and sink. "I know you did everything you could. I know you tried." I swallowed hard. "Please tell me, Dad. I want to know."

Finally, the fortress my father had built around his heart began to crumble. The line in his life's sand started to wash away. My dad began to speak.

He told me about the day that he discovered Sarah and Kathleen were gone. He found the lamb in Kathleen's crib. He never heard from Sarah again.

Dad explained that Sarah's father had insisted that my dad was ill-equipped to care for Sarah and the baby, and that it was in the best interest of the child to give her up. Sarah's father told Sarah and my father that they wouldn't be able to afford the child and they were too young to be parents.

As Dad spoke, the sadness in his voice touched me. I didn't dare move or speak. I was afraid he might stop. But he didn't.

He remembered that it took him a long time to sign his name on the papers to release the child. He said his hand shook so badly that he thought his signature wouldn't be legally binding. No lawyer was present. He wasn't advised of his legal rights; he never received a copy of the documents. Nor was he ever told that he had thirty days to change his mind. He learned all these things later.

After he signed the papers, he never had contact with Sarah's family again. He was positive that Kathleen had been given up for adoption, sure that Sarah's father forced it. For months afterward, he said he felt numb.

He told me that for years he searched for her, but

always came up against dead ends. The adoption records were sealed by the state. Once, he paid a lawyer to petition the court to open the records, but his request was denied. He tried to leave a trail for Kathleen to find him in case she wanted to. Then one day, he just stopped searching. He'd lost hope.

"They told me I'd forget," Dad said. "They told me to put it behind me, to get on with my life." His voice broke.

My heart was breaking, too.

I put my hand on his and stroked it. He looked so fragile. He reminded me of a butterfly trapped in a cocoon. *Is this why he became ill? Was it the years of shame and guilt suffered alone that finally triggered the cancer?* The secret was a cancer all its own.

I stood up. "Dad, it isn't as hard as it used to be to find someone who was adopted. There are services that can help. People do it all the time. Maybe when you were searching for her, she wasn't looking for you. Maybe now she's looking for you, too."

He didn't answer.

"Do you have a photo of her?" I asked.

He gave me a surprised look.

"Do you have a picture of her?" I repeated.

He nodded slowly.

"May I see it?"

He shifted his eyes to the nightstand and picked up the handkerchief from behind the lamp. I stepped forward as he set the handkerchief on his lap and unfolded it. In it rested a small silver picture frame. *So this is what was in the handkerchief.*

Dad handed me the frame. Under the glass lay a black and white photograph of him in a Hawaiian shirt. I recognized the shirt. He still had it. In his arms, he held a baby. Dad was looking straight into the camera with a huge smile. He looked so happy.

I leaned over the photo. "She's precious." Then I looked up. "Do you have any other photos?"

"No. This is the only one. Her family took the rest. I used to carry this one in my wallet."

My head and heart were full. I wondered — had Kathleen ever tried to get in touch with my father? Did she know anything about him? How many times had he been up here alone and pulled out this silver frame? I gave him back the photo. He set the frame on the nightstand and continued looking at it.

"Dad, I'll try to find her."

He turned and held me with his eyes. It moved him to hear that. "Thank you." Then he said, "Michael, there's something I want to show you." His voice was calmer now.

"What?"

He motioned toward the closet door.

"In *there*?" I asked.

"Yes."

I stood up and slid the door open. In the closet were his file cabinets and tax books.

"On the top shelf there's a small blue suitcase," he said. "See it?"

"Yes."

"Bring it here, please." I pulled the suitcase down and laid it on the bed. "Could you open it for me?"

I unlatched it. Inside, something was wrapped in a dishtowel.

"What's this?" I asked, pulling it out.

"You'll see."

Dad watched as I unfolded the towel.

"*Wow*," I said, softly.

Tucked in the cloth rested a wooden angel. She was about ten inches tall from the tip of her wings to her feet. She had black hair. Her robe was blue, her wings golden. In her hands, she held a violin and bow.

"It's beautiful," I said, turning the angel over and examining the wings. "Look at all these little feathers."

He laughed. "Don't look too closely."

"You *made* this?"

"Yes."

"When?" I asked, amazed.

He rested his head back on the pillow. "A long time ago. I was younger than you are." He looked over at it lovingly. "I made it for Kathleen."

Chapter Fourteen - The Angel

The summer after Sarah left, Tom went back to work in a small music shop near the opera house. He had worked there every summer since he was a freshman in high school. It was a good job. In the shop, Tom stocked music, worked the register, and repaired rental instruments that children returned at the end of the school year.

The music shop was owned by a man named Mr. Semmelweiss. He had run it for forty years. Mr. Semmelweiss was a short, barrel-chested man with twinkly eyes, thick forearms, a full head of silver hair, and a good-sized belly, which he blamed on drinking too much beer in his youth.

Entering the shop was like lifting the lid of an old instrument case. The door squeaked when it opened, and the room smelled like wood polish, valve oil, cork grease, and horsehair all mixed together. Hidden behind a burgundy velvet curtain in the back of the store was a workshop. There, when Mr. Semmelweiss wasn't fixing instruments, he worked with wood. He was a wood carver. He had learned from his own father who, according to Mr. Semmelweiss, carved some of the animals on the carousel at Coney Island.

In the corner of the room stood an old carpenter's bench. On it lay chisels, gouges, knives, planes, and woodturning tools, along with all sorts of drippy bottles, cans, and jars full of varnishes, polishes, glue, and paint. Above the bench, on a pegboard wall, files, drills, handsaws, and clamps of various sizes were lined up within reach. On a nearby counter sat a band saw, a lathe, a buffer, and an old Zenith radio in a wooden case with red Bakelite knobs. The sawdust on the creaky hardwood floor looked like it had just snowed indoors. The room always held the wonderfully earthy smells of cut pine, oak, and cedar, which Mr. Semmelweiss jokingly called Eau de Workshop.

The shop was full of Mr. Semmelweiss's carvings, including a child's rocking horse with a finely polished saddle and a music stand tooled with grapes and sheaves of wheat. On the shelves sat an elaborately carved box, a sailing ship with a miniature figurehead, and a doll bed and chairs with tiny posts and legs that he turned and scrolled by hand. Spread out on a table in the corner of the room lay a large nativity that Mr.

Semmelweiss displayed in the front window of his shop every Christmas.

Once, when Mr. Semmelweiss was starting on a new piece, Tom asked him, "What are you making now?"

"Whatever the wood tells me to," he replied. Mr. Semmelweiss believed that the figure was already in the wood. "The carver," he would say, "just has to find it."

When the shop closed for the day and Tom was finished sweeping the floor, he usually joined his boss in the back. Together they would talk, sometimes for hours at a time, about life and sports and books and music. Occasionally, Tom would grab a piece of wood and whittle while they talked and listened to symphonies on the radio. Oftentimes, they would try and guess the title. Mr. Semmelweiss missed only once — and then he claimed that the announcer was wrong.

Mr. Semmelweiss knew all about what happened with Sarah and Kathleen. Tom went to see him soon after Sarah left and told him everything. He never judged Tom, never gave him advice. He just let Tom talk.

One morning, not long after Tom came back to work, Mr. Semmelweiss could see the sadness on Tom's face. He looked like he hadn't slept. Mr.

Semmelweiss walked over to the shelf under his workbench and rummaged through some wood. He grabbed a piece of pine and brought it over to Tom.

"What's this for?" Tom asked.

"I thought you might like to carve something."

Tom shook his head. "No, thanks. I'm not in the mood." Tom had fiddled around with wood before, but only for fun.

"It might do you some good."

"No. No. Thanks, though."

Mr. Semmelweiss looked down at the wood. "It's a good piece." Then he glanced over at the nativity in the corner. "I think it would make an awfully nice angel, if you ask me." He turned the wood over and puckered his lips in thought. "It wouldn't be difficult to make one," he continued. "You could make the wings separately and attach them to the body later. The only hard parts would be the face and hands. But I could help you with those."

Tom gave half a smile. "Thanks for the offer, but I'm not really up for it."

Mr. Semmelweiss set the wood on the workbench and walked over to the crèche. It was a large set with many pieces. Then he picked up a rag and started dusting off the stable.

"I made this for my wife," he said.

Tom eyeballed him. "You did?"

"Yes," he answered. "I made the whole set for her."

"I didn't know that." Mr. Semmelweiss rarely talked about his wife. In fact, in all the years Tom worked there, he heard very little about the man's family. Tom got off the stool and walked over to the nativity as Mr. Semmelweiss picked up one of the Wise Men and wiped it off. "Each year, I'd try to add a new piece," he continued, setting down the figurine. "That's why there are so many sheep." He gave Tom a wink. "Sheep are easy to carve."

Both men laughed.

Then Mr. Semmelweiss looked above the crèche where a host of angels hung on the wall. There must have been at least ten of them. He searched the angels until he spotted the one he was looking for, then carefully took her down. Her robe was painted light blue, her wings gold. Rosy cheeks accentuated a mischievous grin. One eye was winking.

"This was my wife's favorite piece," he said. "She called it *her* angel." He pointed to her head and smiled. "See her halo? It's slipping off." He grinned. "My wife liked that an angel had a slipped halo." Mr. Semmelweiss began to hang her back up. "Carving always helps me forget my troubles. My wife called it my therapy."

Tom smiled at him. He was a good friend for

trying to help like this. "OK," he said. "I'll give it a go. But you have to help me."

Mr. Semmelweiss held back his smile. "What would you like to make?"

"An angel, of course."

That evening, Mr. Semmelweiss helped Tom draw the wings onto the wood, and Tom cut them out. Then he showed Tom how to carve small feathers onto the wings. While Tom worked on the feathers, Mr. Semmelweiss continued with a set of candlesticks he had been working on. For long periods the workshop was quiet, except for the steady sound of sandpaper and chamber music on the radio. From time to time, Mr. Semmelweiss would lean over, inspect the wings, and say, "Very good."

As Tom carved, he remembered a drawing of an angel that hung in his bedroom when he was a child. His father, Cyril, gave it to him just before he left for the war. He had cut it out of a magazine. In the picture, two children were walking through the woods. Behind them stood a guardian angel, her large wings illuminating the path. The angel was playing a violin. Tom used to stare at the picture from his bed and count the number of animals hiding in the forest.

One night, when Cyril was tucking him into bed, Tommy looked over at the picture and asked, "Do all angels play instruments, Daddy?" Cyril smiled as he pulled the sheets up to Tommy's chin. "Not all," he answered. "But I think all guardian angels do."

"Why?"

"Well," Cyril continued, sitting on the bedspread, "as you know, the ways of angels are very mysterious. Only God knows how they help us. But I think that when a child is sad or lonely or frightened, his guardian angel plays on her instrument, and the notes float away. Then the breeze catches them, and the music dances through the stars and makes them twinkle." Tom listened closely. "Then the music wraps itself around the child like this . . ." Cyril reached his arms around Tommy and gave him a tight hug. Tommy giggled. Leaning in so close that his nose was almost touching his son's, Cyril whispered, "It's the angel's music that comforts us."

That summer, Tom continued to work on his angel, and Mr. Semmelweiss helped him with her hands and face just like he said he would. When her face emerged, Tom found himself grinning. It looked as though she was smiling up at him.

"You know what?" Tom said to Mr. Semmelweiss one night as he was working on her robe. "Someday, I'm going to give this angel to Kathleen."

A hint of a smile crossed Mr. Semmelweiss's face.

Then Tom held the angel out in front of him and

spoke to her with a smile. "You will be my baby's little angel." He turned to Mr. Semmelweiss with happy eyes. "How about that?"

"I think she'd like that."

Tom didn't finish the angel at the shop. Over the years, he'd pull it out from time to time and work on it. After he and Shirley were married, sometimes he'd sit at the kitchen table or out on the balcony carving the tiny feathers on her wings or painting her. Occasionally, Shirley would sit beside him and crochet or work on her crossword puzzles. She never asked whom the angel was for. She knew. One day, when the final coat of varnish was dry, Tom glued the miniature violin and bow that he had made into the angel's hands. "There you go," he said. "Now you look like a *real* guardian angel." His angel was finished.

As Tom smiled down at her, he reached into the corners of his mind and slid back in time. With eyes shut, his thoughts transported him to the day he set up Kathleen's crib. Mathilda had bought it at a secondhand store. The crib was white with pink bunnies on its panels and plastic teething strips on the side rails. Tom squeezed the memory. But then another flooded his mind — the tragic day when he first discovered Kathleen was gone.

It was a rainy gray evening in February. Tom had

just returned home from school. It was close to dinnertime. When he stepped into the house, he called out "Hello!" as he usually did, but no one answered. That's odd, he thought. He knew that his mom was out giving a piano lesson and would be back soon. But Sarah and Kathleen should have been home. Sarah would have told him if she wasn't going to be there. Tom stepped into the kitchen. There was no food on the stove. The table wasn't set for dinner. He walked upstairs and opened the bedroom closet to hang his coat. As he reached for a hanger, he noticed a row of empty ones on the rod. Sarah's clothes weren't there.

He hurried over to her dresser and opened the drawers. Empty. He rushed to the bathroom. The counter was clear of Sarah's things. Panicked, he ran back to the closet, where he discovered Kathleen's clothes gone, too. Then Tom darted from room to room, shouting for Sarah and his daughter. He raced outside, but there was no sign of them. The rain was coming down hard now. Drenched, Tom stumbled back into the house, staggered up the stairs, and collapsed onto the floor of his bedroom. Tears streamed down his face as his chest heaved and his mind swirled with questions: *Where did they go? Were they safe? Why did they leave? How can I find them?*

When Mathilda returned home, she found Tom in a ball, sobbing beside Kathleen's crib.

Tom didn't usually let his mind journey to these places. It was too painful. But today, he allowed himself to go there. After a deep sigh, he set down the angel, walked into his bedroom, and shut the door. There he opened his violin case and took out his violin. He tuned it, cradled it in his arms, then began to play as he often did when the thought of Kathleen became overwhelming. His violin was his confidant, his refuge, his balm. As the music washed over him, a tear dripped onto the handkerchief under his chin.

Chapter Fifteen

As I held the angel up to the lamp, the wings shone against the light — like an ornament, I thought. How beautifully it was crafted, each cut, each stroke a sign of a man's love for his child. I handed Dad the angel, and he touched the violin in her hands.

"You know," he said, "Kathleen liked listening to the violin."

"What do you mean?"

"Well, sometimes when she would cry and we'd tried everything to calm her down, I'd take out my violin and play for her. She'd stop fussing right away."

"Did you play for me, too?"

"Oh, yes. You liked it as well." He smiled. "But most of the time you kept on fussing."

We both chuckled.

Dad's voice reached over and said my name. ". . . If you ever find her, would you please give her the angel?"

"Of *course*."

His eyes were moist. The tears made them look even bluer. "And . . ." I could tell he was trying not to cry. "And please tell her I'm sorry."

I leaned into him and smiled. "I will tell her that you love her."

At that moment, I felt strangely peaceful and happy, as if a blanket of pain and unforgiveness had been lifted off me and replaced with compassion and thankfulness for this man. My heart had changed key. Dad and I had a long way to go, but it was a good start.

I picked up the angel and started wrapping her in the towel. Wait, I thought. *She shouldn't be hidden away anymore. Neither should the lamb. There is nothing more to hide. There's nothing more to be ashamed of.* My heart lifted.

"How about we put her on the tree?" I suggested.

"If you'd like."

"No, what if *we* put her on the tree together?"

He squinted at me.

"I mean it, Dad. Could you get downstairs if I help you?"

He shook his head.

"What if I carry you?" I asked, excited with my plan.

"Michael . . ."

I handed Dad the angel and scooped up the lamb. Then, before he could argue with me, I put one arm around his shoulder, another under his legs, and picked him up, quilt and all. "Hold on!"

"Careful."

"Don't worry," I said, laughing. "I won't drop you."

Cradling him in my arms, I walked carefully out of the bedroom and down the stairs. Carol had just changed the record on the stereo when we entered the living room.

"Papa!" Christopher shouted. Karen held him back.

Mom stood up quickly. "Tom!"

"It's all right, Sug," Dad said.

My smile filled the room. "Dad wanted to make sure you all weren't stealing his presents."

As I set him down on the couch, Mom rushed over and fussed with the quilt, and Carol started to cry. After Dad was settled, he stared at the tree. He looked like a child again, standing in front of the Christmas windows at Marshall Field's. Like a great magnet, the tree held him in its grasp. No one spoke as my father's eyes scanned the branches. On them hung the pink ornament and the rattle, the shepherd and the plaster bride and groom, the love letters and the toy soldier.

There were other ornaments, too — a pair of baby shoes, the little white box that held Mom's pearl earrings, wine corks with dates and names of places written on them, an egg carton bell from Tom and Shirley's first Christmas tree, a handprint made at school out of plaster of Paris, corsages of dried carnations and gardenias from my parents' wedding anniversaries, and the hook I wore when I played Captain Hook in third grade.

Mom sat down on the piano bench, and Dad turned his eyes on her and brightened. Her sitting there reminded him of when they first met at the nurse's Christmas party many years before. The memory came rushing back to him so clearly, and he closed his eyes to hold on to it. And then, with his eyes still shut, his thoughts took him far away from this room, the cancer, the pain. He was in 1958, sitting with Shirley on a crayon-green lawn in front of the hospital where she worked. The breeze ruffled the grass. She was wearing her nurse's uniform, white stockings, and a starched cap with a pale green *K* on the corner for the Kaiser School of Nursing. It was four months after they met. Tom surprised her at the hospital with a picnic basket on her lunch break. As they sat on a blanket, he pulled off petals from a daisy. But before he started to ask if she loved him or loved him not, he made sure that the daisy had an odd number of petals.

I set the lamb on the tree skirt next to the crèche. Then I found a hook in the ornament box and attached it to the back of the angel. I stood in front of the tree for a few moments searching for a place to hang her until I spotted just the right branch. Carefully, I hung the angel, letting go of it slowly to make sure that the branch didn't sag. It supported her well.

Christopher climbed out of Karen's lap and curled into Dad's. Carol sat in the rocking chair as Mom joined my father. I sat down beside him and put my arm around his shoulder. Dad leaned his chin on Christopher's head and stroked his hair. Together we all looked at the tree. The white lights were shining. The Douglas fir still had all its needles. And Heifetz was playing Tchaikovsky on the stereo.

Afterword

One-and-a-half months later, my father passed away at home. In those final weeks of his life, he was able to both give and receive an unalloyed love that sustained and consoled us. Carol, my mother, and I were with him in the last hours when his breathing slowed and weakened. The exact moment of his death was difficult to ascertain. It was like deciding when the sun has finally sunk beneath the ocean horizon on a clear sunny day. When he left us, the Christmas tree was still up for him. On his desk upstairs, the bills were all lined up for my mom. After his death, when we were going through my father's things, I brought the violin case to Mom and showed her the framed photograph of him and Kathleen. In the light, we discovered what looked like lip marks on the glass where he had kissed it.

My family celebrated many more Christmases in my parents' home until one year my mom decided that it was just too big for one person and put the place up for sale. When she left the house, the nails for the stockings were still in the mantel, the hardwood floor lightly stained from where the Christmas tree used to stand. Mom downsized to a condominium. Even though it was June when she moved in, the first thing she did was figure out where the Christmas tree would go.

Every December, I still drive to Joe's Tree Farm to get my tree. Usually Christopher and his wife and kids come with me. Christopher gives me a hard time when I walk around the entire lot searching for the best one, but I know he's just kidding. My grandkids are old enough now to help cut it down.

After I get the tree home and on the side of the house, I drive out to the cemetery. It's not far. I go alone. At this time of year, the cemetery is dotted with poinsettias in green foil paper, and pine wreaths with red bows rest on some of the headstones. When I reach my dad's plot, I am usually winded from the walk, so I rest a bit. Then I get down on my knees and clean away the leaves and pull the weeds. While I'm working, I tell Dad how the family is doing and which teams are playing in the bowl games this year. Dad's grave is in a sunny spot. I'm happy about that.

Eventually, I stand and begin setting up what I

brought along with me — a small Douglas fir. Joe Jr. never charges me for Dad's. I wrap a towel around its base and hang a few plastic bulbs. Sometimes, I throw popcorn in the branches for the birds. When I'm finished, I sit for a while in silence.

Today, the ornament box lives in my house, in the closet of the guest bedroom. And every year, the day after Thanksgiving, Karen tells me to be careful of my back when I climb the ladder and take it down. Like me, the box has lost most of its shape. The sides aren't as flat as they used to be. It's a little heavier than it was the year before. Karen says I should buy a new sturdier one, but I can't seem to get around to it.

Christopher's children help me decorate the tree now. They know all the rules for ornament hanging. And they know their stories. They learned them all — even about the lamb and the wooden angel, though they never saw them. For the angel and the lamb only stayed in the ornament box a few years after I first discovered them. They now belong to another — to a blue-eyed woman with black wavy hair who found out late — but not too late — of the man who loved her and thought of her every day of his life.

Acknowledgments

I am deeply grateful to the following people for their support, assistance, and belief in this book: Heidi Fisher, John Wiley, Jr., Debbie Reynolds, Donald Light, Janis Donnaud, Tia Graeff, Brian Halley, Jason Anderson, Connie Sutherland, Carol Velazquez, Phillip Irwin Cooper, Doug Grude, Matt Phillips, Jay Hakerem, Eva Schinn, Marion Beach, and most of all, Piotr Konieczka, whose unending encouragement and support made this possible.